You See, What Happened Was...

Introduction by LawDog, Edited by Kortnee Bryant

Raconteur Press

Per My Last Email

Copyright © 2023 by David Matsui

A Zoo of a Day

Copyright © 2023 by Aelth Faye

High Noon on Bugscuffle Colony

Copyright © 2023 by Andrew Milbourne

Pointing Appendages

Copyright © 2023 by Peter Delcroft

The Last Flight of Samson, the Giant Fiberglass Bull

Copyright © 2023 by Ted Begley

Andrew Spurgle's Day in Court

Copyright © 2023 by Jay Dee

A Clinic in Gaslighting

Copyright © 2023 by Moze Howard

You Stand Accused

Copyright © 2023 by Sarah Arnette

Love & A Bit of Disorder

Copyright © 2023 by Elaine Canyon

Lead The Way

Copyright © 2023 by TC Ross

The Colorado Incident

Copyright © 2023 by Sherri Mines

To Whom it May Concern

Copyright © 2023 by Kortnee Bryant

COPYRIGHT

All rights reserved.

No portion of this book may be reproduced in any form without written permission from the publisher or author, except as permitted by U.S. copyright law.

Cover art and Design by Cedar Sanderson

Contents

Introduction	VII
1. Per My Last Email David Matsui	1
2. A Zoo of a Day Aelth Faye	3
3. High Noon on Bugscuffle Colony Andrew Milbourne	14
4. Pointing Appendages Peter Delcroft	41
5. The Last Flight of Samson, the Giant Fiberglass Bull Ted Begley	59
6. Andrew Spurgle's Day in Court Jay Dee	77
7. A Clinic in Gaslighting Moze Howard	81
8. You Stand Accused Sarah Arnette	103
9. Love & A Bit of Disorder Elaine Canyon	121

10.	Lead The Way TC Ross	146
11.	The Colorado Incident Sherri Mines	167
12.	To Whom it May Concern Kortnee Bryant	190
Also From Raconteur Press		194
Call To Action		195

Introduction

Baen Books has the famous—or infamous—Joe Buckley. Raconteur Press has Andrew J. Spurgle.

I originally conceived the character of Spurgle as a *tabula rasa* for our authors, a "creation of each individual author, with the only required characteristic being his glorious, glaring incompetence." Spurgle would be the thread that would tie each story in the "Your Honor, I Can Explain" anthology together, and to add some levity to what is ordinarily a pretty dry subject.

Mr Spurgle's popularity amongst our authors was rather unexpected, as is his—dare I say—global reach. He has been making appearances in some unusual places.

I was asked some time ago if I had expected Andrew J. Spurgle to be popular as he is, and truth be told, I really didn't. I had thought that given the peculiar restriction of his character, we'd have trouble getting enough stories to fill one anthology. As you can tell (since you're currently holding the second volume of a trilogy), this was obviously not the case.

What about an obnoxious, bumbling clown-shoe of a character makes him so popular? In short, I think everyday life does. Every one of us has had to deal with someone whose rampaging clueless incompetence has made the day, or the job, so much harder (and unnecessarily so) than it needed to be. We all have stories of that one particular individual whose very name induces heartburn or a headache.

Being creative people, it is naturally incredibly satisfying to write a story—loosely based, you understand—about that person, and have them receive their proper comeuppance: to give them the just desserts they so richly deserve without the risk of the criminal charges (or stay in the cackle factory) that would come with doing so in real life.

I hope that reading these stories is as cathartic to the reader as it was for the various authors.

Without further ado, here is Book Two of The Spurgle Chronicles: *What Happened Was...*

Enjoy!

LawDog

Tiny Town, Texas

2023

Per My Last Email

David Matsui

Per my last email:

Lt. Spurgle is not to draw pentagrams or anything else on the decks.

His efforts predictably resulted in absolute failure. Somehow, his scribblings transmuted the reactor into a giant squid. Squid started smashing while screaming about being god. The Marine contingent disagreed.

Repairs will be extensive.

2 YOU SEE, WHAT HAPPENED WAS...

A Zoo of a Day

Aelth Faye

It was a slow Wednesday, and Tragedeigh was polishing the bar for the fourteenth time in two hours when a new face walked in. Well, most of a face. The poor human had clumps of graying hair missing, burns all over him that were covered liberally in liquid bandage and greasy ointment, and a complexion that could have come straight from the grave. Tragedeigh was used to unusual characters, this being an interstellar hub bar, but this man took the cake.

"A Moon Launch, please. On the rocks."

Tragedeigh had been bartending for the past decade and knew better than to ask questions from a man looking this bad, but she still raised her eyebrows at the uncommon request. She dug at her belt for the biometric key as she glanced around the bar to ensure no one was close enough to jump her. Finally, she opened the safe containing the most expensive liquor this side of the Andromeda. Made from grapes grown in genuine moon dust and fermented in a diamond cask, this stuff was rumored to taste like unicorn sparkles and rainbows. Well, that was the polite analogy. The less polite one involved a phrase about star farts and two unicorns.

She mixed up the drink in a genuine-Earth amber glass, also stored in the safe, and set it down gently in front of the man. He grabbed it and downed it in three gulps. She swallowed hard and grabbed her rag. Time to polish the bar again, this time nearby. There was a story here and she was darned well going to hear it!

Four drinks later, each one costing more than a month's wages for the average worker, the man was ready to talk. Not yet slurring his words, he was leaning on the counter and moodily eyeing his empty glass. The light from the Edison bulbs glinted off it in interesting patterns. Tragedeigh knew, because she'd done the same thing more than once.

"Ever walked into work expecting a decent day and it turns into a tragedy?" the man asked, his voice both hoarse and gravelly. He blinked in surprise at the sound of it, then shook his head.

"Ask me about the day I was born sometime," she groused, gesturing to her name badge.

He blinked at her, then the badge, and a faint smile crossed his face. "Fair point."

"But do go on," she responded. "It's been a boring day for me, and evidently the same can't be said for you."

"That's one way to put it. You ever been to the zoo?"

"Any zoo, or that one that's been in the news lately?"

"That one. 'Mott's Selection of the Strange and Unusual Creatures Found Among the Spheres.'"

Tragedeigh blinked. She'd never heard anyone actually say the full name of the place before. Whoever had come up with that title deserved to be forced to say it fifty times per day for the rest of his or her life.

"Yeah, once. It was all right."

"We got this new guy about a month ago with a ton of brilliant ideas. His name is Spurgle, of all things. Now, don't get me wrong, some of his ideas are great. We've gotten ten times the visitors that we normally get during the slow season. But gosh darn it, this guy is a bumbling idiot when it comes to day-to-day stuff!"

"I would normally ask if he set off a bomb," Tragedeigh joked, "but in this case, it looks a little too close to the truth."

"You're telling me," he muttered. "Can I get another one of these?"

Tragedeigh looked at his hefted glass and tried to remember which drink had been the last one. Was it a starlight surprise or a genuine-Earth whiskey soda? She mentally flipped a coin and got him the latter, as it was far easier to mix.

"One of his bright ideas was having teens help out around the zoo as part of a scholastic enrichment program. They come in for the day, feed animals, shovel shit, and get a shiny badge and an even shinier certified letter they can take to the school of their choice that counts as a half credit. Great idea, everybody loves it, and it means less work for us. In theory."

He took a swig of his drink, grimaced, then set it on the table. "Today, the owner decided we were going to include an educational video along with the actual work. All well and good, but the boss let Spurgle order the video. I'm not sure what it was supposed to be about, but the bits I saw involved a pair of scantily clad ladies, giant spiders, and a swarm of Martian carrion beetles."

There was a chuckle from someone farther down the bar, and Tragedeigh abruptly remembered she was still on the job, and glanced around to see if anyone else needed a drink. Two beers and a mug of molasses later, she was back to polishing the bar and waiting to hear the fallout.

"Needless to say, the chaperones demanded to see the boss, and I got caught in the middle of it as the most senior employee on site. I kicked the blame back to Spurgle, who promised to fix everything. Me, being an idiot, believed that he might be able to do it, so I didn't protest."

The man took a deep breath, then continued, "He suggested that the kids feed the chimeras. I've warned him the chimeras had been fed twice already today, but did anyone listen? Of course not! The chimeras glutted themselves on food and the females instantly went into heat, and, well, you can guess what happened next. It made that little video that everyone was trying to forget look like a kiddie birthday party.

"Now, the enclosures at the zoo are safe. They're designed to hold the animals no matter what happens under any circumstances, even if the power goes out. But that's only assuming that the people working at the zoo aren't idiots. And remember how I said we've been having teenagers help out at the zoo lately? At least one of those teenagers was an idiot. Someone scratched their initials into the crystal plating on the inside of the chimera enclosure. This would still be fine...if they hadn't also decided to stuff an empty beer can into the electrical box."

The man started to run a hand through his hair, then winced and thought better of it. "Long story short, there were sparks, and the boss and I sprinted for the tranq guns, and we got all but one of the chimeras down within thirty seconds. A record, if I do say so myself."

"Then we discover that idiot Spurgle grabbed the wrong tranq gun. Mind you, they're sorted by size and color-coded with little infographs beneath them, showing which animals they can be used for, and the gun for the Plutonian animals is a sparkly gold color. But no, this idiot grabbed the first one that came to hand, which was an elephant gun, of all things."

"So you had a dead chimera on your hands?" Tragedeigh hazarded.

"Yup. And if you know anything about Plutonian animals, you'll know what that entails."

Tragedeigh wracked her brain, trying to remember her interstellar biology class from two decades ago. "Are they the ones that explode?"

"You got it in one, lady. And they don't just explode, they explode in a rainbow spray—for chimeras, anyway—of *acid*. Half the kids were in the splash zone, and so was I. To make matters worse, this chimera just happened to be near the sabertooth enclosure when it happened."

"I'm guessing the everything-proof enclosure isn't Plutonian-acid proof, is it?"

"Of course not!" the man replied, rolling his eyes. "But I'm gonna need another drink. Got any suggestions? Something that won't burn going down and isn't too sweet."

"A sour Neptune?" she offered. It wasn't as pricey as the drinks he'd been ordering, but it was a favorite of her customers.

He nodded and she mixed it up. He left the table, heading towards the bathrooms, and she kept an eye on the cameras, just in case. She didn't think he was the type to split before he paid his bill, but doing a DNA trace off cups was a pain in the butt, and the interstellar police really didn't like being called for such petty stuff.

She asked the customers still seated if they wanted anything else, and mixed up two drinks and grabbed a cider. Just as she was starting to worry, she saw the human leaving the bathroom in the vid feed and returning to the bar.

The man took a sip of his drink, and his eyes widened. "That is good!"

"So what happened next?" a featherfolk nearby asked, voicing Tragedeigh's thoughts.

"The gate to the elephant enclosure next door got spattered with acid, too. All the commotion had caused the elephants to be a bit concerned, and when the gate started sizzling, one of the bulls charged it."

Tragedeigh winced. So did the featherfolk who had asked.

"What next, or dare I ask? Whales? Snakes?"

"Fire ants," the man said, staring at the table in distaste. He pushed his thumb down, squishing something. "I thought I had killed all the buggers. Sorry."

Tragedeigh blinked. "Why does a zoo have fire ants?"

She absentmindedly ran a hand over the bun her waist-length brown hair was pulled up into. The thought of ants of any kind made her skin crawl, but the idea of insects infesting her hair...she shuddered and forced herself not to think about it.

"Another one of Spurgle's brilliant ideas," he complained, running a hand through his hair, as if in sympathy to her thoughts, then wincing as he touched the burns on his head.

"'We need to widen our selection and make it more educational,'" he quoted in a nasally voice. "And my idiot boss listened in all the worst ways.

"In an effort to not die, I grabbed a fire hose and started spraying myself and everyone down. It got the fire ants off, but it didn't do good things to the acid burns."

Tragedeigh could envision the water hitting the acid and causing it to spread, just making it larger and worse. That wasn't a comfortable thought.

"In another of Spurgle's great ideas, he had decided to be proactive on the safety side of things and invite some OSHA guys to tour the place, citing that it was extra safe and could be highlighted in their 'Safe Workplaces' newsletter. Of course, today was the day they decided to visit."

There was a snort from farther down the bar, and Tragedeigh saw a drink atomize out of the corner of her eye. She threw a bar cloth at the Martian who had tried to laugh while drinking his cider.

"Needless to say, the pictures they started taking are not likely to make it into the 'Safe Workplaces' newsletter. The boss and I sprinted for the elephants, and Spurgle decided to talk to the OSHA guys, since he couldn't go near the elephants. Why, you ask? Because a few days ago, he gave them manta feed which made them very sick. And you know elephants' memories are legendary."

"So is OSHA's," someone murmured, making Tragedeigh smile.

"Somehow, in the midst of all of this, we had all forgotten to announce that the zoo was closed. We only discovered this when a troupe of kindergartners and their three teachers came strolling out of the butterfly house straight into the midst of all this. Spurgle, to his credit, ran over to them and ordered them all away. Unfortunately, he took the diplomatic approach and didn't just say that we were in the middle of a mess. The teachers got the idea that we were just doing a training exercise—and they thought that the sabertooth eyeing them was actually domesticated.

"I jumped for the tranq gun I had dropped not far away, not even caring at this point which animal it was intended for, and shot the giant cat, but not before the teacher had advanced on it, hand extended for it to sniff.

"My next task was to fish the teacher's severed hand out of the sabertooth's mouth..." the human said as delicately as a man of his type could. There was a muffled squeak from someone at a table near the door, but Tragedeigh ignored it. If you were in a bar listening to a guy explain why his skin was peeling off, you had to expect stuff like this to have happened.

"I sent Spurgle off for ice, because you gotta keep stuff like that cold until the surgeons get at it, and he came back with a ginormous slushy cup, which we plopped the hand into. Then Spurgle and the boss shoo the teachers back into the butterfly house and tell them to stay put until the medics get there. At this point, Spurgle announces he has a family emergency and is going to have to go home.

"I'm normally a nice guy. I don't drink often, I don't cuss much. If I'm walking down the street, I'll move out of your way, you know. But *this*...this is the last straw. Still, I take a deep breath and ask him what, exactly, the emergency is. And what do you think it was?"

"His house was on fire?" a nearby Martian hazarded.

"Naw, knowing this guy, it's going to be, hmm...maybe his cat got caught in his bed curtains," a featherfolk offered.

"I like that one," Tragedeigh said, filling another mug with beer for a human customer who had just come in. "I'm gonna guess that his pet snake got heatstroke."

"I dunno what we're guessing about," the newest customer said, "but I'm gonna say car battery exploded."

One of the other customers brought the newest one up to speed while the battered human continued his story.

"Good guesses, but any of those would have been better than the excuse he had. Turns out, his score for an event in that new zombie game had slipped below twenty-five and he needed to go home to play a few rounds because he had promised his girlfriend the loot box and armadillo armor he was supposed to get for scoring in the top twenty-five."

"The *hell*?" someone exclaimed.

Tragedeigh agreed, though she would have used different words. Probably more colorful ones, actually. The more she heard about Spurgle, the more pathetic she thought him.

"Unsurprisingly, that's when I lost it. I started yelling at him and telling him that this whole damned mess was his fault and so forth. Now I'm not proud of it, but damn it, someone needed to say it!

"But does Spurgle take it to heart? Of course not! Instead, he calls over one of the OSHA guys and very politely says that he thinks my mental health might be suffering and he's worried about me. Of course my mental health is suffering! I'm about to flipping explode!

"Mind you, we still have two flipping elephants loose at the moment and Spurgle can't go near them. So the boss is trying to wrangle one of the elephants and the OSHA guys are arguing about whether any of them have the proper credentials to step in and help with the other one, and here I am covered in blood and acid, holding a severed hand in a slushee cup. And this idiot OSHA guy is telling me that I need to get a psych eval because of my 'unstable mental outburst' before I can touch any of the animals."

"Then Spurgle, with another of his bright ideas, realizes that we can have one of the kids help. They all have signed waivers to be part of the educational program and took the required safety courses. So he grabs a tall kid and hands him a bucket of peanuts and sends him towards the elephants. Only problem is, he picks a featherfolk. And those guys all smoke constantly. And elephants do not like fires."

"Hey, man." The featherfolk spoke up. "We haven't adapted to breathing nitrogen properly. The smoke is medicinal."

The human waved a hand in the featherfolk's direction. "Sorry, didn't mean any offense. My specialty is animals, not sentient beings."

"None taken. Just trying to educate the masses."

"Anyways, one stampede later, we have shit flooding the walkways from a burst silo, four more enclosures are breached, and these blasted little fire ants are still pouring out of their enclosure. Worse yet, now OSHA is on the phone with the interstellar emergency services. Not the planetary ones, oh no. They decide to take it all the way to the top.

"The medics finally arrive, and I can finally hand off the slushie cup with the teacher's hand in it to them. I can at least use my hands, though they're itching to punch that stupid little balding OSHA guy because he still won't let me do anything and is insisting that I need to provide proof of my last health exam before I can return to work.

"And then the interstellar cops arrive at the scene. But do they land nicely on our helipad? That would be too easy! Instead, they decide to land right in the middle of our aviary. So now we have a few decapitated birds and feathers everywhere and a few more blood spatters adding to the mix. And, of course, the birds are now escaping the aviary, since there's a ship-sized hole in the top fencing.

"We had just imported some new birds, including a few of the lethes they just discovered in the Hercules jungle. Anyone know about those?"

"Venomous birds that will knock you out," the Martian nearby said with a shudder. "My sister imported one of those. Talk about cruel."

"Ding ding, we have a winner! Right you are, sir or madam: they bite people and knock them out. And guess who they go for first? The guys in green—which would be the interstellar cops. So they're just passing out on us while trying to shoot these stupid birds and the two little kindergartners managed to escape the butterfly house and they're chasing after the dumb things so the cops are trying not to shoot them. And then the power goes out across the whole zoo."

"What?"

"The power. Turns out the main power line is buried underground. And all that shit sludging down the walkways managed to seep into the ground, and it was acid enough to eat through the conduit and short out the lines."

"What next?" Tragedeigh asked. "You discover a bomb somewhere? The backup generator explodes?"

The man laughed. "The backup generator just fizzled a little before it went into emergency shutdown mode, too. No, that was basically the end of it. We all started trying to clean up the mess and get everyone taken care of and the animals all back inside. Until another group of OSHA guys came decked out in full PPE and they shooed us out of there and said they'd take care of it."

"That sounds like a hell of a day," the newest last human customer remarked.

"But why are you here and not at the hospital?" Tragedeigh asked. "I feel like OSHA would have required a checkup after all that."

He laughed bitterly. "Another of Spurgle's brilliant ideas. He convinced the boss to switch to a different insurance with better coverage. There was only going to be a two-day lapse in coverage, and surely nothing would go wrong during those two days, right?"

"Oops," someone murmured.

"Basically. So emergency services are covered, but nothing else. No hospital or clinic visits until the day after tomorrow. Here's hoping all the goo they smeared on me stays on until then."

"Wow. I guess your only consolation is that Spurgle's gonna have to suffer, too, eh?" the featherfolk put in.

"And that's the cherry on top of this bloody mess. The bastard passes out because he got bit, right? When the medics get to him, they say he's in a coma because he has a sensitivity to Lethe venom. He'll be fine, but he'll just sleep for a few weeks instead of a few minutes. But coma care counts as emergency services, so he gets the royal flipping treatment at no cost while I'm here covered in cheap medical goo. And the lucky bastard is going to sleep through the cleanup and paperwork and leave us poor suckers working overtime to clean up this place. If we even still have a place to clean up, after the interstellar police and OSHA are done."

"Wow. Just...wow," Tragedeigh said. "That's a hell of a story. Normally, I'd clear your tab for you for that kind of entertainment, but I'm afraid that's out of my budget. Let me at least get you another drink, this one on the house."

He waved a hand dismissively. "Naw, don't worry about it. That's the only good part of this whole thing. This is a qualified traumatic event and our mental health plan, which didn't get changed so it's still active, covers a lot. It doesn't only cover the normal therapists and psychs and stuff; it also includes social stress-relief activities such as massage, VR arcades, and, wait for it, all bar tabs within seven days of the event. Speaking of which, I could use some friends tonight, so a round for the house on me!"

The man handed over a metallic blue card engraved with a healthcare-sounding name, and Tragedeigh ran it through the reader. Sure enough, it was accepted, showing a mind-bogglingly high limit for qualifying expenses, which it verified this was. Tragedeigh poured out drinks for the house and then one for herself. That had been a hell of a story, and all good stories were best discussed over a drink. Besides, she'd never had a chance to try a Moon Launch before.

"To Spurgle," she said, raising her glass.

The man raised his drink, as well. "Long may he sleep."

High Noon on Bugscuffle Colony

Andrew Milbourne

Hawk knew she was in trouble the second she and Miss Corbett disembarked from the transport.

Captain Walker was waiting for them in the terminal. That had never happened before. While Miss Corbett was pulled into a tight, loving embrace by her overjoyed mother and father, and then subsequently mobbed by reporters, Walker shot Hawk a look that was equal parts annoyance and long-suffering exasperation as he wordlessly motioned for her to follow him.

"Sir, what...?" Walker cut Hawk off with a raised finger on one hand while he pinched the bridge of his nose with the other. Hawk hoisted her rucksack onto her back and silently fell in behind her superior, wheeling her rifle case along behind her as the two Rangers threaded their way through the Governor Greg Abbott Interstellar Spaceport's perpetually crowded passenger terminal.

When they exited the terminal building and reached the curbside pickup zone, Hawk realized that she was in deeper trouble than she thought: there was a hovercar waiting for them. Not a Ranger-issue pickup hovertruck, but a sleek, expensive sedan with tinted windows. The kind that executives and politicians get chauffeured around in when they want to be "discreet."

"Sir?" Hawk ventured again, but Walker's only reply was a quiet mutter that Hawk thought sounded like "not here." The driver opened the rear passenger door for the Rangers and then deposited Hawk's luggage in the trunk. It wasn't until the hovercar had pulled away from the terminal and had begun threading its way towards downtown New Austin that Walker finally spoke.

"Ranger Hawk, we received a rather angry comm from the Bugscuffle Colony Council yesterday. Would you care to explain why you shot Constable Spurgle in the hindquarters?"

"Well, you see, sir, what happened was…"

"No, no, I don't want you to tell me," Walker interrupted. "I want you to think *real* hard and try to come up with an answer that is satisfactory enough to *maybe* allow you to keep your badge. Because when I say 'we' received it, I mean the Governor. Not the Governor's office. Not his secretary. The Governor himself. On his personal comm line. On a Sunday afternoon. While he was at a barbecue. With his grandchildren."

"Oh."

"Yeah, 'oh.' Which is why we are on our way to the Governor's Office, where he, the Chief, the Assistant Chief, *and* the System Attorney are all waiting to hear your explanation of what exactly happened on Bugscuffle and how a slug from your personal sidearm wound up in the Constable's posterior."

"Long story short, sir: the stupid son of a bitch had it coming."

Hawk winced, closed his eyes, and pinched the bridge of his nose again.

"Knowing you, Jacinta, I don't doubt it, but for the love of God, *do not* tell them that!"

***

This must be how a supercow feels when it realizes that it's walking into the slaughterbarn, Hawk reflected as some political flunky or another led the two Rangers through the Governor's mansion to the Most Important Room in the Solar System. Just as Walker had warned, the Governor of the Solar System of New Texas, the Chief of the New Texas Rangers, the Assistant Chief of the New Texas Rangers, and the System Attorney of New Texas were waiting. No sooner had the two Rangers been admitted and introduced to the politicians than the System's Attorney—a self-described Peoples' Progressive who reminded Hawk of an extra-sleazy used hovercar salesman—exploded all over the room.

"In all my years of serving the People of this once-great Solar System," the SA proclaimed, "this is, without a doubt, one of the most egregious displays of governmental abuse and excessive force that I have ever witnessed!"

"Ever witnessed?" the Chief snorted. "Cortez, we all know you didn't witness a damn thing, and you wouldn't visit a place like Bugscuffle if your life depended on it. Can't risk getting mud on those nice taxpayer-funded boots of yours."

"Gentlemen!" the Governor barked, silencing both longtime rivals before they could start slinging insults—or worse—at each other yet again. "Ranger Jacinta Hawk," he continued, "your reputation precedes you."

"Thank you, sir."

"That wasn't a compliment!" Cortez sneered.

"That is enough, Alejandro!" the Governor barked. "I may not be able to fire you, but we both know damn well that I can make your life plenty miserable. Now this whole mess already has me in a mighty bad mood and your attitude is not helping one bit, so if you want me to make your life as much a living hell as I can manage, then please, *please*, continue running your mouth. Otherwise, kindly sit down and be silent. *Comprende, Señor?*" Cortez gave Hawk a sour look as he reluctantly returned to his chair.

"Now then," the Governor continued, "Ranger Hawk, as I was saying, you have caused my office, and myself personally, one massive headache. I was enjoying a pleasant weekend with my grandchildren when I received a *very* angry call from one Colony Constable Andrew J. Spurgle of Bugscuffle Colony regarding the Annabelle Corbett kidnapping. You were the Ranger assigned to that case, correct?"

"Yes, sir." Hawk knew full well that the Governor had known the answer to that question long before she had departed for Bugscuffle Colony in the first place.

"Constable Spurgle called me personally this weekend to complain about your conduct in resolving that case. He claims that you...what were his exact words?" The Governor retrieved an open notepad from his desk and looked it over. "Ah, yes. You demonstrated utter contempt for his authority and for the law in general; flagrant disregard towards the safety of him, his deputies, Miss Corbett, and nearby civilians; executed suspects in cold blood after they had surrendered; and deliberately shot the Constable himself in the, ahem, in the buttocks." He set the notepad back down on the desk and looked Hawk square in the eye. The Ranger did an admirable job of not squirming or shirking back under his intense, angry glare.

"Now, Ranger, I trust you understand how these accusations make you personally, your department, and my administration look?"

"Yes, sir. I do, sir."

"And I trust that you deny them?"

"Most of them, sir."

"...Most of them?" the Governor's eyebrows shot skyward as an evil-looking smirk spread across Cortez's face. The Chief and Assistant Chief shared a click nervous glance. Walker went pale and he almost pinched the bridge of his nose again, but caught himself just as his hand began to move. "So...you are admitting that at least some of the Constable's accusations are true?"

"Yes, sir. I did, and still do, hold Constable Spurgle in utter contempt, and while I did shoot him in the ass, that was not deliberate on my part."

"So you...accidentally shot the Constable?"

"Yes, sir."

"'Accidentally,' as in you had a negligent discharge?"

"No, sir. 'Accidentally' as in the Constable let his hind parts get between the muzzle of my sidearm and my target while I was engaging said target, sir."

"And your target was…"

"The no-good, wannabe-Communist varmint that was trying to shoot me, Miss Corbett, and the Constable, sir."

The Governor slowly sank into his plush overstuffed leather chair and began massaging his temples, trying to ward off a migraine, while the Chief and Assistant Chief exchanged exasperated looks and Captain Walker was unable to stop himself from pinching the bridge of his nose. System Attorney Cortez looked like he wanted to start tearing Hawk a new one, but wasn't quite ready to risk the Governor's wrath again just yet.

"Okay, Ranger." The Governor sighed at long last. "Why don't you tell us exactly what happened, starting from the beginning?"

"Well, sir, what happened was…"

∞

Hawk had arrived on the tiny world at the edge of the Solar System of New Texas known as Bugscuffle Colony four standard days after the terrorist group that called itself "The Beto Brigade of the People's Revolutionary Liberation Army" had kidnapped Miss Annabelle Corbett. The kidnapping itself had been rather simple: a half dozen "freedom fighters" had sped up in a hovervan as Annabelle had emerged from a salon in downtown New Austin, blasted her bodyguard (along with her personal assistant and a trio of civilians who had been in the wrong place at the wrong time) all to hell and gone with ancient Kalashnikov-pattern slugthrowers, then grabbed Miss Corbett, pulled a bag over her head, tossed her into the back of said hovervan, and sped away. Six standard hours later, Miss Corbett's grandfather, one of the wealthiest supercow ranchers in the solar system, had received a ransom demand for fifty million pesos, in cash, of course, along with a proof-of-life video.

Nothing else about the case had been simple since.

That first comm had been traced to a coffee shop with a pretentious reputation just west of the University of Texas at New Austin's campus, but by the time New Texas DPS's Rapid Response team had arrived, the Beto Brigade member that had placed the comm was long gone. And predictably, none of the shop's employees or management had seen anything or was willing to play ball. And then all subsequent communications with the "freedom fighters" (as they demanded to be called) had been traced to Bugscuffle Colony. That included a live comm between Mr. Corbett and Annabelle that could not have been faked. Which meant that despite all of the spaceports being placed on high alert to the point of being all but locked down, the kidnappers had managed to transport Miss Corbett offworld. And so Ranger Hawk had found herself on a government-chartered express transport from the Governor Greg Abbott Interstellar Spaceport to Bugscuffle Colony's first and only landing complex.

There was nobody waiting for Hawk when she disembarked. That was unusual: tradition going back centuries to Old Earth said that a member of local law enforcement would meet a Ranger when they arrived in their jurisdiction, escort them to the local HQ or command post, and give them at least a cursory briefing or update on whatever case had brought them there. But there was no one from the Bugscuffle Colony Constabulary at the port, not even a secretary or a hired hovercar. And speaking of hired transport, the Bugscuffle Colony spaceport complex was so small and bare-bones that it didn't have so much as a single rental hovercar available, let alone an actual rental company anywhere close to onsite. And the one taxi driver that was parked outside the tiny passenger terminal declared himself "off-duty" when Hawk tried to hire him. No amount of asking, pleading, badge-flashing, or outright threatening would sway the driver, whose attitude grew exponentially more abrasive and condescending by the second.

Hawk was just about ready to exercise her authority as a Ranger to commandeer the vehicle when an older gentleman who'd overheard the commotion approached and offered to take Hawk "into town," since he was headed in the same direction. Hawk displaying her badge and holstered sidearm and informing him of her occupation only made him more insistent that she accompany him. Hawk looked him over: he seemed friendly enough and didn't strike her as duplicitous or having any ulterior motives, and it was several hours' walk to "town," AKA the only major city on Bugscuffle Colony that had, rather creatively, also been named "Bugscuffle." So Hawk had tossed her rucksack and gun case into the bed of the older gentleman's pickup and climbed into the passenger seat.

"Don't think I've ever heard of a Ranger coming 'round these parts before," the driver, who'd introduced himself as "Curt," remarked. "Guessin' you're workin' a case?"

"I'm afraid so," Hawk replied.

"And I'm guessin' you can't talk about it?"

"Afraid not."

"Thought so. Been there, done that. Workin' jobs I can't talk 'bout, that is."

"You ex-law?" Curt let out a hearty guffaw.

"Naw. Ex-Navy."

"SEALs?" Curt's guffaw turned into an outright belly laugh.

"Not hardly! Interstellar maritime patrol. Spent thirty standard years goin' all over the damn sector on PM-7 Orion IIIs."

"And I'll bet that includes a few places that you absolutely, positively, swear up-and-down-and-sideways on a stack of Bibles you never went anywhere near, right?" Hawk gave Curt a knowing wink.

"More 'n a few, an' that's all I'm gonna say on *that* particular subject, unless you wanna shoot yerself an' then me for sharin' classified information."

"I'd rather not do that."

"I imagine you got some good stories, too."

"Oh, yeah. Hell, just last month, I got sent all the way out to Krasnoyarsk."

"*Krasnoyarsk?* That's way inside Orlov Combine territory!"

"It's the Sovereign Star Kingdom of Romanova now, remember?"

"Eh, it'll always be the Combine to me. Now what in hell were you doin' out there?"

"What else? Running down a fugitive."

The pair traded old war stories for the better part of an hour until Curt turned his hovertruck onto Bugscuffle proper's Main Street and stopped in front of a squat and ugly single-story building that had a big sign which read "Colony Constabulary Headquarters" hanging next to the door. Hawk thanked Curt for the lift as she climbed out of the vehicle. To her mild surprise, Curt insisted on pulling her luggage out of the bed. "Yeah, you're a Ranger, but I was raised back when chivalry was a thing in this system," he explained, and then adamantly refused any form of compensation for the ride. Hawk gave him a wave as he drove off before heading inside.

The lobby was drab and depressing, sparsely populated by cheap-looking furniture that was a half-century out of style. Dominating the room was the enormous desk set towards the back wall. Manning the desk was a matronly-looking older woman with long, silver hair who looked to be the most bored secretary in the entire solar system. She eagerly looked up from her holopad as Hawk approached.

"I'm here to see the Constable," Hawk said as she set her gear down on the floor.

"I'm afraid he is out of the office for the next few hours," the secretary said with a long-suffering sigh. "Is there anything I can do to help you while you wait?" Hawk wasn't sure if the attitude was directed towards her or the unexpectedly-absent Constable, so she kept up her friendly professionalism.

"He should be expecting me. I'm Ranger Jacinta Hawk out of New Austin." She flashed her badge at the secretary. The old woman let out a long groan, swiveled around in her chair, and hollered into the back of the building.

"Hey, Mac!" she bellowed in what could be only described as a "Mom Voice." "The Ranger is here!"

A very long, very loud, and *very* colorful string of expletives exploded from the back of the building, followed in relatively short order by an extremely pissed-off Deputy Constable that Hawk knew had to be Mac before she saw the nametag stitched to his uniform shirt. Mac was an older man, though several years younger than the secretary, with short red hair, a rather impressive handlebar mustache, and an odd accent that Hawk couldn't quite place.

"You're Ranger Jayhawk?" Mac demanded.

"Hawk. Jacinta Hawk."

"Got ID?" Hawk obliged him, fishing her credentials out of her shirt pocket and presenting them. He gave them a quick but critical look before nodding politely at Hawk.

"J. Hawk. Figures the dumbass'd mess that up, too. Anywho, whatever your name is, you're the one I'm supposed to haul in back and toss in a cell."

"I'm sorry?" Hawk said, her tone deadly serious. She not-very-subtly moved her hand towards her holstered slugthrower.

"Yeah. The ever-brilliant Constable Spurgle ordered me to arrest you for 'interfering with an active investigation' or some such bullshit." The tone that Mac used when uttering his boss's name was the same one most people would use when referring to a particularly vile specimen of bacteria or vermin. "Only I'm not gonna do that because I'm not an incompetent glory-seeking asshole, it will piss off the incompetent glory-seeking asshole who gave me that insanely idiotic order, and, more importantly, I don't have a fucking death wish!"

"I appreciate that." Hawk relaxed her gun arm. "May I ask where Constable Spurgle is at the moment?"

"Oh, you certainly may! But you might wanna sit down before I tell you."

"Just tell me, Deputy."

"Okay, but don't say I didn't warn you. Constable Dumbass has the whole fuckin' force, save for yours truly and Joan here, out at the old Scrumshaw place. That's where those Beto Bozos have holed up with Miss Corbett."

"You're sure that's where they are?"

"Oh, yeah," Mac nodded. "We, and by 'we' I mean myself and the two other competent deputies in this joke of a department, tracked 'em there less than a standard day after they arrived. Wasn't all that hard since they were practically braggin' about who they were and what they were up to, bragging to everyone who'd listen. But ol' Constable Void-Brain specifically ordered that nobody, and I mean *nobody*, inform New Austin or anybody else. Couldn't risk somebody like, say, a *New Texas Ranger* showing up and stealing his spotlight."

"The reporters, Mac," Joan reminded him. "Don't forget to tell her about the reporters."

"Reporters?" Hawk asked weakly.

"I was just about to get there, Joan. Yeah, the one group he *did* inform was every single fuckin' media affiliate on this Godforsaken rock. He wants the whole fucking system to see how awesome he is when he singlehandedly rescues Miss Corbett. Only his idea of a 'rescue' is to drive right up to the front door in our armored hovercar and order the Beto

Bozos to release their hostage or else he will huff and puff and blow the house down like he's the Big Bad Fucking Wolf. Idjit has the whole thing planned to go down at 'High Noon,' too. No shit, that's what he said. 'Come High Noon today, all of New Texas will know the name 'Constable Andrew J. Spurgle!' And he's damn right that they will, because come High Noon, that dumbass is gonna get people killed. And if we're all really, *really* lucky, it'll only be himself."

"You're shitting me, Mac." Hawk groaned. "Please, *please* tell me that you're shitting me."

"Nope." Mac drew the 'o' out and popped the 'p.' "Wish to God I was, but unfortunately you've got…" He checked his wrist chrono. "Just over one standard hour to get your ass out there and try and stop one hell of a clusterfuck."

∞

Mac couldn't go with her. His orders from Spurgle notwithstanding, he was the only Deputy left in town after the Constable had "gone off to get himself and Miss Corbett and probably the whole damned department killed and who knows who else along with them!" and *somebody* needed to be on hand to deal with any other emergencies that cropped up. He could, however, call for help. That help turned out to be Curt, who was apparently Mac's good friend, drinking buddy, and commiseration partner. The older man was more than happy to give Hawk another ride in his hovertruck. And it turned out that his hovertruck was damn fast, almost certainly illegally modified, but Hawk wasn't about to look a gift horse in the mouth, so she kept her damn mouth shut while she (quite literally) held on to her hat as Curt raced down the packed dirt road towards the old Scrumshaw place at a remarkably dangerous speed.

After several hair-raising minutes, a dot appeared on the horizon. Said dot rapidly grew into a cluster of vehicles just in front of a rundown split-rail fence and gate that sort of crossed the road. Dominating the scene was an ex-New Texas Defense Force APC that had been painted jet black and had "Bugscuffle Colony Constabulary" stenciled on the front, rear, and both sides in big, gold block letters along with a matching shield emblem. Behind the APC was a full dozen hovervans painted up in the liveries of the system's major news networks. Hawk spat a few choice expletives in Comanche. Mac hadn't been exaggerating.

At Hawk's instruction, Curt stopped the truck about fifty meters from the vehicles. No sooner had the hovertruck jerked to a halt then Hawk leapt from the cab and sprinted for the fence, snatching the gene-locked case containing her carbine as her boots hit the dust. A young man clad head-to-toe in black tactical gear with "DEPUTY CONSTABLE" stenciled across his body armor in the same gold block letters that were on the APC moved to intercept her, but stopped short when she flashed her badge.

"Oh shit," the scrawny-looking lawman groaned. "The Constable isn't gonna like this."

"Deputy," Hawk growled, "What the Constable likes or doesn't like is the least of my concerns at the moment. Now where is he?"

"Where else?" The deputy pointed towards the thick knot of reporters and holocams set up between the fence and the APC, and the pudgy-looking figure standing behind an honest-to-goodness podium that had been erected in the middle of the road. "He's hogging it up for the cameras."

"Is..." Hawk started. "Is he...?"

"Wearing his dress uniform during a tactical raid?" the deputy finished wearily. "Yep. Has to look the best for his moment of glory, after all. And before you ask, yes, Ranger, this momentous occasion is being broadcast live."

Hawk snarled something that would have made the deputy blush if the poor man had understood Comanche, then shoved her way past the lawman and made a beeline for the press conference. Spurgle hadn't noticed Hawk's arrival or her interaction with his subordinate; he was far too focused on delivering what he was certain was the most important speech of his long and soon-to-be-prestigious career to pay attention to much of anything.

"...And with this afternoon's swift and decisive action against these vile terrorists," Spurgle bloviated, "I and my courageous deputies shall prove once and for all that law, order, and justice are no strangers to Bugscuffle Colony, and that we shall no longer tolerate outlaws, scofflaws, gangsters, fugitives, thugs, hooligans, or crooks using our peaceful world as a hideout or a base of operations from which to plot and hatch and launch their nefarious schemes! The galaxy's ne'er-do-wells will learn that law and order have a name here on Bugscuffle, and that name is Constable Andrew J. Spurgle!"

On the other side of the holocams, the media types were stifling yawns and groans. They had been listening to Constable Andrew J. Spurgle jabber on and on and on and on for—one particularly bored holocamraman checked his wrist chrono—nearly forty standard minutes. The entire group was collectively wondering when the pudgy gasbag would finally shut up and give them the thrilling show he'd promised their networks. A few technical personnel noticed Hawk's rapid approach, realized who and what she was, and eagerly braced themselves for a spectacle.

They were quickly disappointed. Hawk moved from one network hovertruck to the next, quietly sticking her head and her badge inside and politely requesting that they terminate their live feed immediately. All but two complied, since everyone, even the news media, knew that inviable rule of New Texas: Do Not Antagonize A New Texas Ranger. The two producers who did refuse quickly changed their tune when Hawk summarized the situation and made some not-particularly-vague references to charges of interfering with a criminal investigation, conspiracy, and accessory. Only once Hawk had confirmed that all the live broadcasts had stopped (and promised to unleash a special brand of hellfire upon the offending parties if any were resumed) did she shove her way through the crowd and approach the podium.

"Call off the raid!"

Spurgle's proud and arrogant grin abruptly transformed into an angry snarl as his face turned beet-red.

"How dare you interrupt me and question my authority! Who do you think you are?"

"I'm Ranger Jacinta Hawk, Company Alpha out of New Austin." She pulled her badge from her belt and flashed it at Spurgle, then turned around just long enough to give the reporters and the holocams a clear look at it. "And per the Governor's orders, I am now in charge of this situation."

Spurgle made a sound that was a combination of a laugh and a snort.

"Very funny, little lady. Now you've had your joke, so go on home and let us grown-ups do our job."

"Do I sound like I'm joking, Constable?" Hawk's tone was hard as steel and all business. "I am now the ranking officer in charge of this incident, and I am hereby ordering you to call off your raid and return to your headquarters..." She spun on her bootheels and addressed the media. "... And I hereby order all of you to shut down, pack up, and go home immediately!"

"Nobody's going anywhere!" Spurgle bellowed at the media. "Keep those holocams rolling!" He turned his blustery anger towards Hawk. "You think you can just show up in my jurisdiction and throw your weight around and bark orders like you own the place?"

"You're damn right."

"And what makes you think you can do that? On whose authority?"

"Oh, now, let's see: the Governor, the Director of the New Texas Department of Public Safety, the Chief of the New Texas Ranger Division, the New Texas Legislative Code, and the ancient code and tradition of the Rangers dating back to Texas on Old Earth."

"And none of those people are present here, little lady!" Spurgle sneered. "This ain't New Austin or New Texas Prime! This here is Bugscuffle Colony! *I* am the ranking authority here, which means that what *I* say goes, and *I* say that *I* and my deputies are going to rescue Miss Annabelle Corbett in..." he paused to check his wrist chrono, "...precisely three standard minutes and twenty-two standard seconds!"

"You do that and you'll get Miss Corbett killed! Along with your deputies, yourself, and any members of the media stupid enough to go with you!"

Hawk hadn't thought it possible, but Spurgle's face somehow managed to turn an even deeper shade of red.

"Are...did...are... Did you just *threaten* me?" he sputtered, spittle spraying from the corners of his mouth.

"No, I'm just reminding everyone, yourself included, that you just announced your intended raid on the kidnappers' hideout, including the planned time of said raid, live to every major media network in the solar system! Which meant that everyone in the solar system has likely seen it, and that includes the kidnappers!"

"So?"

"So? *SO?*" Hawk felt her professional mask beginning to slip, but in that moment, she didn't care. "So you just told them you're coming, genius!"

"You don't know that! The Scrumshaw place has been abandoned for years. It has no power connection. They can't possibly have a holonet connection."

"Can't possibly... Spurgle, were you born an incompetent, idiotic sack of supercow shit, or did you have to take lessons? Do you really think that they couldn't have brought in a power generator, or have spare power cells or a dime-store solar charger for their PADDs? They have proven remarkably competent, *far* more competent than you, let me point out, they are heavily armed, they have a hostage, *and they know you are coming!* You go charging through that gate today, and your name is going to be known all over the solar system as the man who got Miss Annabelle Corbett killed and most of his deputies massacred!"

"They wouldn't dare harm Miss Corbett!" Spurgle sneered. "She is far too valuable to them alive! And our tactical assault vehicle's armor is more than capable of defeating their primitive slugthrowers. The raid *will* launch as scheduled, and if you open your mouth again or make any move to stop it, little lady, then I *will* order my deputies to arrest you for obstruction of justice, interfering with my investigation, *and* aiding, abetting, and collaborating with Miss Corbett's kidnappers!"

"You're joking," Hawk scoffed. She glanced around, and the smug grin she'd allowed herself faded from her face. Most of the media types were staring in slack-jawed disbelief at Spurgle. No lawman was foolish enough to treat a New Texas Ranger that way! But while two of the deputies were backing off and looking at their boss like he'd completely lost his mind, the others—and there were at least a dozen of them—were slowly advancing towards her with their maser rifles not quite pointed at her, but angled close enough to make their intent obvious.

Hawk swore under her breath. This was *not* how this was supposed to go down. And she did *not* want to get into a gunfight with fellow peace officers, no matter how arrogant and stupid their boss might be. She sighed, clipped her badge back to her belt, and looked Spurgle dead in the eye.

"Don't say I didn't warn you. And you all," she turned to the media, "if you're smart, you'll either stay here or else get your footage from way far back from the farmhouse. You stick close to the raid, you'll just make yourselves into targets." And with that, Hawk shoved her way back through the crowd and took off running down the road.

Straight back to Curt's waiting pickup.

"I'm gonna hazard a guess and say things did not go according to plan," Curt quipped as Hawk leapt into the passenger seat.

"Damn fool is gonna get everyone killed," Hawk snarled. "Dumbass sicced his deputies on me when I tried to take charge, and the morons actually followed his orders."

"Ah, yep," Curtis sighed. "Real shining example of competent law enforcement, our Constabulary is."

"How well do you know the old Scrumshaw place?"

"I know it well enough. Ol' Pete used to let us hunt on it back in the good ol' days."

"Can you get me around back behind the farmhouse before Spurgle and his team make it out there?"

"I can surely try. Hang on to your hat, Ranger!"

∞

Curt did indeed know the Scrumshaw property well, or at least well enough to go blasting through the rises and dips in the terrain at breakneck speed. The way the cab rocked, bucked, and leapt violently back and forth and side to side reminded Hawk of the time Francis talked her into riding what he'd called a "gentile" bull. There had been *nothing* gentile about Hawk's one and (if she had anything to say about it) only bull ride, and there was even less calm about Curt's wild off-road driving. But she managed to retain her carbine and her wits (and her breakfast) until her unofficial deputy *finally* brought his hovertruck to a halt behind a grove of trees.

"Farmhouse is through there." He pointed towards the trees. "About a hundred meters."

"Any cover?"

"Sagegrass probably hasn't been cut in a few years. Other than that..." Curt shrugged. Hawk muttered a curse under her breath as she leapt from the truck. This morning just kept getting better and better.

"Keep it running, and get ready to drive out of here even faster than you drove in. I'll probably be coming in hot with Miss Corbett."

"You got it, Ranger." Hawk was already running into the trees.

Curt was right: the sagegrass on the other side of the grove was well above waist-height. And in a long-overdue twist of good luck, the wind had picked up enough to rustle the grass, *and* it was blowing towards the house, which meant that Hawk was able to move quickly through the brush without being noticed by anyone who might be keeping watch from the farmhouse.

Hawk was ten meters away from the decrepit single-story farmhouse's back door, still well hidden by the sagegrass, when she heard the APC crawling up towards the front of the building. She checked her wrist chrono. That had taken a hell of a lot longer than she'd expected. Spurgle had taken his sweet old time launching his "assault." She figured he'd wanted to look good for the camera crews that he'd no doubt ordered to keep pace with him, probably while he stood in the commander's hatch holding a pose that he thought made him look dramatic but actually just looked silly. (She couldn't know it, but she was correct on all counts.) The APC came to a halt when she was just over three meters from the door.

"*ATTENTION, MEMBERS OF THE PEOPLE'S REVOLUTIONARY LIBERATION ARMY!*" Spurgle's electronically-amplified voice boomed from the APC's public-address system. "*THIS IS CONSTABLE ANDREW J. SPURGLE OF THE BUGSCUFFLE COLONY CONSTABULARY! YOU ARE HOPELESSLY SURROUNDED, OUTNUMBERED, AND OUTGUNNED! I HEREBY ORDER YOU TO THROW DOWN YOUR WEAPONS, RELEASE YOUR HOSTAGE, AND SURRENDER! YOU HAVE ONE MINUTE TO COMPLY! SHOULD YOU FAIL TO HEED MY ORDERS, THEN I AND MY*

DEPUTIES SHALL UNLEASH AN ASSAULT UPON YOU SO OVERWHELMINGLY FEROCIOUS THAT YOUR PATHETIC MINDS WILL NOT BE ABLE TO COMPREHEND WHAT IS HAPPENING! YOU HAVE SIXTY SECONDS! MAKE MY DAY!"

Hawk choked back a groan, then froze as the back door eased open. Two figures, both male, came creeping out onto the back porch and down the stairs onto the narrow strip of neatly-trimmed sagegrass that bordered the house. One of the men was holding a Kalashnikov-pattern slugthrower rifle, and the other had a Kalashnikov slung over his shoulder and a stubby olive-green tube in his hands. The tube was just over a meter long and about ten centimeters in diameter, and Hawk felt her blood turn to ice as she recognized it: a Hebei-manufactured Chengde DZB-55 anti-armor rocket launcher. Designed to neutralize main battle tanks, the weapon would utterly annihilate the APC and everyone in it. And the shrapnel from that explosion would kill or maim who knew how many of the media types.

"Don't shoot, Constable!" a voice called from inside the farmhouse. "We're surrendering! Give us a minute to cut our hostage loose and we'll come out with our hands over our heads!"

"GOOD CALL! YOU HAVE TWO MINUTES!"

Hawk worked out the set-up in half a heartbeat: the kidnappers' surrender was nothing more than a delaying tactic to give their rocket team time to get into position and take out the APC. After that, the rest of the group would probably gun down any surviving deputies, and maybe the media types, too. Hawk thought they'd want the media types to live, get them on their side, make them look like heroes or something, but then again, they seemed trigger-happy enough to not really care about collateral damage. And while Hawk didn't much care for the media in general, and *really* didn't care for Constable Andrew J. Spurgle, she still couldn't let any of them get hurt. So she did the only thing she could do: she shouldered her carbine, flicked the safety off, and stood up.

"New Texas Ranger!" she barked. "Throw down your weapons and throw up your hands!"

The two kidnappers instinctively spun towards her, their eyes going wide as their brains struggled to figure out where the hell she had come from. The one with the rifle reacted first and began lifting the muzzle towards Hawk. The Ranger snapped her sights onto his chest and double-tapped the trigger. Two 7mm Miculek polymer-tipped rounds pulped his heart. He staggered backwards, his finger tightening on the rifle's trigger in a death grip as he fell. He dumped the magazine in a single wild burst that stitched across his partner's legs and chest as he fell. The man with the launcher screamed as he fell forwards. He must have hit the trigger because he and his friend's body abruptly disappeared in an ear-splitting blast and a geyser of dirt and burnt sagegrass.

"*WHO IS SHOOTING? CEASE FIRING! I ORDER YOU TO CEASE FIRING!*"

The back door flew open. Another kidnapper, this one a woman with a maser pistol held next to her head and pointed skyward like in a bad holofilm, ran out onto the back porch to see what had happened. Hawk was already running up the patio steps. The lady kidnapper started to bring her pistol down. Hawk shot her point-blank in the face and shouldered her falling corpse aside. The door was swinging closed thanks to its sprung hinges. Hawk kicked it back open with her heel and dove into the farmhouse.

The inside of the farmhouse was just as decayed as the building's exterior. The ceiling had come down in a few spaces, the floor sagged in spots and floorboards were buckled in others, and adult-size holes had formed (Hawk wasn't sure how) in most of the interior walls. Which gave Hawk a clear view of—and clear fields of fire on—nearly everyone in the building.

Annabelle Corbett was hiding under the rickety old bedframe in the back corner furthest from the door. The bedframe was topped by a filthy old mattress and a ratty old blanket. A bucket was set up at the foot of the bed. One end of a thick chain was locked to the footboard while the other end was connected to the manacle on Miss Corbett's ankle.

The remaining kidnappers were all in the front of the house, still in their firing positions by the doors and windows. A few had begun turning their attention to the rear of the building.

"New Texas Rangers!" Hawk bellowed. "Drop your weapons!"

Not one of them dropped their weapon. They all pointed them towards Hawk. One fired, blowing a hole in the back wall with his maser rifle, but Hawk was already moving. She bodily planted herself between the kidnappers and Miss Corbett and set to work with her carbine, firing and shifting targets until all the threats she could see had been neutralized. She hadn't gotten all of them: she'd seen a few of them move. But she held her position; no way was she letting any of them get between her and Miss Corbett. Hawk dropped into a crouch, swapped magazines, and waited: she knew they'd come looking for her soon enough.

She didn't have to wait long. One flung himself through a hole in the wall at her ten o-clock: she put a shot through his eye. Two more came through the door and were put down with a pair of double taps before either got a shot off. One more leapt through the door right in front of her, firing blind. He died with bullets through his heart and a third between his eyes.

It was all over in less than a minute. As the echoes of gunfire faded, Hawk moved over to the bed and crouched down next to the trembling Miss Corbett.

"Annabelle?" she said, not quite as quietly as she would have liked since she still had to be heard over Constable Spurgle, who was still screaming orders to "cease firing this instant!" into the APC's PA system. "Annabelle Corbet? My name is Jacinta Hawk, and I am a New Texas Ranger. I'm here to bring you—"

Hawk didn't quite manage to get the word "home" out before Annabell Corbett exploded out from under the bed, threw her arms around the Ranger, and buried her face against Hawk's chest as she started sobbing. "Ma'am, we're not exactly out of the woods yet. Can you walk?" Miss Corbett nodded quickly, pulling herself away from Hawk and taking several quick, deep breaths to get herself under control.

"I can walk, ma'am, but..." She gestured at the manacle around her ankle.

"Where's the key?"

"I don't know. They told me that they stored it somewhere, but I don't know who has it or where it is."

"Let me take a look at it..." A quick glance at the manacle revealed that the lock was a simple, absolutely ancient mechanical design. "No problem. Give me just a second...." Hawk fished a lockpicking set out of her duster's pocket and, saying a silent thanks that Spurgle had *finally* shut up, set to work. It only took a few seconds to rake the lock open and get the manacle off Miss Corbett's ankle.

Hawk kept her poker face off as the manacle came free; the cold, unpadded steel had rubbed the skin raw, and blood was oozing from the swollen joint in several places. It did not, thankfully, look infected, but Hawk wasn't about to take any chances. She fished a compact first-aid kit from another duster pocket and, after a quick apology, began tending to the wounds. Miss Corbett bit back a pained hiss as Hawk applied the antibiotic spray, and winced a little as the ranger wrapped a sterilizing bandage around her ankle, but she didn't complain at all.

"Okay, let's get you up..." Hawk helped Miss Corbett to her feet, then waited as Annabelle tested her ankle. She grimaced a bit, but it was obvious that her leg would take her weight. "All right, let's get going..."

"No one is going anywhere!" Hawk and Miss Corbett turned to find Constable Spurgle marching into the farmhouse, one hand hovering above the long-barreled Deagle Mk LV slugthrower pistol holstered cross-draw on his hip. "You..." he pointed at Hawk, "... are under arrest!"

"You have got to be kidding me," Hawk groaned while Miss Corbett gave the Ranger an aghast glare.

"I thought you said you were a New Texas Ranger!"

"I did, and I am. He's just an idiot." Spurgle didn't ignore her insult so much as not notice it, because he'd already wound himself up into a self-righteously indignant rant.

"You big high-and-mighty types think you can just rocket in from New Austin and throw your weight around and take over *my* operation and steal *my* recognition and *my* glory? Well, you are sadly mistaken, Miss Ranger Jayhawk! *You* are not the law here; *I* am the law! And I am hereby placing you under arrest for interfering in a Constabulary investigation, murder, reckless..."

"Murder?" Hawk and Miss Corbett exclaimed together.

"Yes, murder!" Spurgle sneered. "Ranger Jayhawk executed the kidnappers in cold blood *after* they had agreed to surrender!"

"That's not true!" Miss Corbett protested. "They faked surrendering and were going to blow up your tank and shoot you..." Hawk gently elbowed her in the side.

"Forget it, ma'am. He's rolling."

"Murder, reckless endangerment, and whatever other charges I can think of! You'll be behind bars for a long time, do you understand me, Jayhawk? A *very, very* long time! And don't count on your friends in New Austin to come and rescue you, either. We don't provide luxuries like offworld comm calls to scum like you! No, you will rot away while you rue the day that you crossed Constable Andrew J. Spurgle! This will be a warning to *anyone* who dares challenge the authority of..."

Hawk was just about to lose the battle to keep from rolling her eyes when she thought she saw a shadow move in the hole just behind and to the left of Spurgle. Were her eyes playing tricks on her or...the shadow moved again, and a large revolver poked through the hole.

"GET DOWN!" Hawk spun and tackled Miss Corbett to the floor an instant before the surviving kidnapper cranked off a shot. Spurgle let out a frightened yelp and tried to draw his slugthrower, but in his panic forgot to undo his holster's retention locks, so he stood there in the center of the room yanking futilely on his pistol while a gunfight was erupting around him.

Hawk rolled off Miss Corbett and came up in a crouch, one hand pinning the ex-hostage's shoulders to the floor while the other drew her own sidearm and punched it out towards the shooter. The kidnapper poked her head out, looking for Hawk. The Ranger put her ancient 1911's gold bead front sight on the kidnapper's forehead and applied the necessary weight against the trigger...

...Just as Spurgle gave his sidearm, still stuck in its holder, an especially vigorous yank. The incompetent lawman knocked himself off-balance and spun himself around—directly into Hawk's line of fire. Hawk noticed him a microsecond too late. Her pistol's sear tripped, the hammer fell, the firing pin struck the primer, and a .38 Super hollowpoint was launched down the barrel and out of the muzzle. The slug struck Spurgle in the side of his left gluteus, just missing his overly-long holster, transited through the muscle formation, exited and then immediately entered his right gluteus. It exited the right gluteus almost perfectly mushroomed, and careened forward until it struck final kidnapper directly in her right eye. She was dead before she hit the floor.

For his part, Spurgle immediately fell over backward and then instantly leapt back up, both hands clamped firmly on his now-bloody posterior.

"YOU SHOT ME!" he screeched. "YOU BITCH! YOU SHOT ME! You can add attempted murder of an officer of the law to your list of charges, Jayhawk!" Then he realized what had just happened and what he had just said. "I'M HIT! OH, GODS, I'VE BEEN HIT! I'VE

BEEN SHOT! I'M DYING!" He grabbed at his comm. "CONSTABLE DOWN! CONSTABLE DOWN! I'VE BEEN SHOT! I'M HIT! MAYDAY! MAYDAY! CONSTABLE NEEDS ASSISTANCE!! OH GODS, IT HURTS!"

Hawk didn't wait around to see what happened next or how Spurgle's deputies were reacting. She threw her sidearm back into its holster, snatched her carbine up off the floor and slung it across her back, then lifted Miss Corbett into a bridal-style carry and bolted out the farmhouse's back door, down the porch steps, and through the sagegrass.

Curt and his pickup were still waiting right where Hawk had left them. The oldtimer waited just long enough to get Miss Corbett buckled into the passenger's seat and for Hawk to jump up unto the bed before pinning the throttle to the floor. The ride out was even worse than the ride in, but Hawk wasn't about to complain. Ninety standard minutes later, they were back at the spaceport. Twenty standard minutes after that, the chartered transport was breaking atmo on its way back to New Texas Prime.

∞

By the time Hawk finished her report, the Governor was vigorously massaging his temples, System Attorney Cortez was staring slack-jawed at the Ranger, both the Chief and Assistant Chief were putting on tremendous poker faces, and Captain Walker had his chin tucked against his chest while he pinched the bridge of his nose hard enough to leave fingerprint-shaped bruises. For several long standard minutes, no one spoke until the Governor finally broke the awkward silence.

"Ranger Hawk, you do realize that there will be a thorough investigation into this incident."

"Yes, sir."

"And that does not concern you?"

"No, sir. I am confident that the testimonies of Miss Corbett, Deputy Mac, Joan, and Curt will corroborate my statement. And per the System Attorney's new policy, I was wearing my department-issued holorecorder at the time, and had it recording from the time I arrived at Constable Spurgle's roadblock-slash-press conference and kept it recording until after our transport lifted off from Bugscuffle Colony. I transmitted the footage to Ranger Headquarters prior to reaching the first Transit Point."

The governor shifted his attention to Captain Walker and the two Chiefs. "Gentlemen?"

"Ranger Hawk did indeed transmit her holorecorder footage of the incident two days ago. We forwarded it to the System Attorney's Office as soon as we became aware of the seriousness of the situation."

The governor frowned and crossed his arms as he swiveled in his chair to face System's Attorney Cortez.

"Alejandro?"

"Uh... I was unaware that said recording existed...but I will personally locate it and ensure that you have a copy to review as soon as possible, sir!"

"You do that. Now, then, Ranger Hawk, Gentlemen, thank you for your time this afternoon. Be safe out there." The Rangers took the dismissal for what it was and took their leave of the Governor. The Chief and Assistant Chief were chauffeured back to the Department of Public Safety Headquarters complex in one hovercar while Walker and Hawk were consigned to a second, far less luxurious hovercar.

"Hawk," Walker said after a few minutes, "don't tell anyone I said this, but you're right."

"About what, sir?"

"That stupid son of a bitch did have it coming."

"Permission to speak freely, sir?"

"I'm gonna regret it," Walker sighed, "but yes, permission granted."

"I told you so."

"Shut up, Hawk."

"Yes, sir."

"And wipe that smug look off your face. It's unbecoming."

"Yes, sir."

Pointing Appendages

Peter Delcroft

The door leading into the front of the butcher shop slammed open, revealing an angry Cadmorian in a loose blue jumpsuit. Volarin's heads bounced around on his shoulders, turning this way and that to take in the room. One of their people was watching the front counter to ensure the meeting wouldn't be disturbed. Beyond that, the business was empty.

Volarin walked behind the counter and lifted the trapdoor on the floor, revealing a ladder leading into the basement of the shop. He knew that at least ten other captains of the now-nearly defunct Quinxit Defilers were going to show up for this rendezvous—as long as they had survived to get here, of course.

The shop they were in was, thankfully, quiet.

Ever since *that* man had entered their lives, quiet had been a forgotten memory, like light in a black hole. Chaos and death would be a more accurate description of Volarin's recent weeks. No blight so terrible had ever been inflicted on the galaxy like the arrival of *Andrew Spurgle* on the galactic stage.

Volarin ditched his plasma pistol with the "worker" behind the counter. He didn't like it, but at a meeting like this, emotions would be running hot, so he saw sense in the rule. No one needed to die over flared tempers or hurt feelings. Volarin climbed down the ladder, then hurried towards the only source of light down the hallways. His entrance into the chamber cut off what seemed to be a quite heated discussion from what he had heard walking up.

"Sit down, Volarin," one captain who had arrived early spat at the newcomer, the venom apparent in his voice. Krokun was a bulky Omnikin, with dark green and blue mottled spots on his scaled skin. Said spots darkened when he was mad, and they were nearly black at the moment.

Volarin straddled one of the empty seats, adjusting himself until he found a decent perch. The sigh that escaped him was like a death rattle. He met each captain's eye before he launched into the bad news.

"Sadly, we were forced into a nasty position and lost a shootout to a Federation patrol. Twenty-two fighters in total and two full starships."

Volarin kept his face neutral once he was done speaking, trying to watch their reactions. Anger and frustration were painted across nearly every face. He reached across the table to grab a bottle of depressant and a glass, only to have his appendage snatched by Krokun, who bounded up from his seat to commit the assault. The table came up to meet Volarin at an alarming speed before Krokun dragged him across it and slammed him onto the floor on the other side.

Volarin kicked and punched, using all his strength to fend off his attacker. Cadmorian versus Omnikan usually came out in the mottled scaled skin's favor, but Volarin was a crafty pugilist. A well-placed blow sent Krokun sprawling, and both captains on instinct reached for their belts. When both came up pistol-less, each grabbed at the chair sitting toppled between them and ripped off a leg. Movement in his peripherals pulled Volarin away from lining up a blow.

"ENOUGH!" bellowed Fendaliss, a Zoarc with no dorsal fin, who stepped forward to put himself between the two combatants. The lean fishman turned to regard Krokun, speaking with a quiet intensity. "I understand your anger, but usually we save this for the Federation, or at least rival sects."

Fendaliss turned to regard Volarin now, the same intensity redirected. It was like watching a searchlight illuminate a prison yard for how it spooked the crooks around the table as it momentarily passed over them on the way to stopping on Volarin. "We are all angry. We all want revenge. Killing each other won't get us there, even if you've been provoked."

By the time he finished, the other captains had stepped in to assist him, and Volarin and Krokun had been escorted to new seats. Each was planted as far across the table from each other as possible.

Krokun adjusted himself at the table, grabbing one of the only unbroken bottles left on the fine oak surface. Volarin couldn't help but notice it was the vintage he had intended to sample, but he swallowed his anger and let it pass. The big man swilled back a large enough gulp to knock out Volarin and chuckled. He then belched loudly, and spoke. "Fine. He better have a good excuse for losing that much to the Spurgleites, or he gets some new holes to ooze from."

Spurgleites—Volarin hated the name—was the term the galactic media was using to describe those who called themselves his followers. As if he was their leader, or even capable of the quality! In truth, they acted in his name, with no noticeable command structure or figureheads beyond their "savior from the tyranny of the elite." Wherever Spurgle was, none but a few of them knew.

If only the common peoples amongst the stars knew who Spurgle really was: a doddering buffoon, a confident idiot who somehow continued to evade all pursuers through sheer luck and stupidity.

Fendaliss finally sat down in his seat once everyone else was settled, gesturing to Volarin. "Can you elaborate on how you lost the ships?" Heads around the room turned, almost as one.

Volarin didn't think the fool would attack him again, so he stood up, grabbed the only unbroken glass on the table and collected an extra bottle from the side of the room. He poured himself a few fingers and sat back for the experience. A long pull followed by the standard shivering—the after-effect the depressant was famous for—and Volarin was ready with his tale.

"Spurgle wasn't there when we arrived at what was supposed to be his ship; instead, we found a derelict with partial vacuum. When we breached the vessel, it was just more of his followers, most of whom we can no longer say are his acolytes. A few even signed on to the Defilers after we captured them. The others are putting in calls to family for ransoms." He paused, letting the words hang over the table. A chorus of groans and moans echoed out on hearing his news. He dodged one drink cap, thrown by Krokun, who was immediately given his last warning by the table, then continued when the complaining subsided.

"There were little, or sometimes large, semi-functional creations left all around the ship. When we questioned the former followers, they claimed Spurgle had described devices from his homeworld, things he—a great saboteur—had used on previous jobs. Apparently, they were integral to his 'work.'" Volarin took another pull from his glass, and his words slowed for a moment as he continued. "Things like a device that looks like a smoke stick but is actually a concealed plasma launcher, or an 'anti-alien' aerosolized spray. Also, some ground vehicle he called an 'Aztin Martian' that could fire petroleum from its exhaust ports while ejecting passengers with the touch of a button. Regardless, none of the things he made worked. In fact, the only thing they did was injure us *and* his own people and prevent them from escaping with him." When Volarin got a few puzzled looks, he brought up the ship recordings on his projection device.

In the first video, an obviously modified smoke-stick contraption blew an Omnikan follower's arm off when he pointed it at a Defiler marine boarding the ship. The video then cuts to a group of followers coughing and wheezing in a cloud of "anti-alien" spray. Volarin pointed out the canisters which laid near the acolytes' feet and seemed to be sparking, all the while pouring out greenish gas.

Fendaliss raised a concerned voice from his side of the table. "Wait, that spray can looked aerosliz—" The video screen went white as the spray finally caught on fire from a spark, creating the illusion that those in the room were some sort of unfortunate momentary sentient candles.

Volarin paused the video. "The folks left alive were mighty pissed to find out his true colors after he skedaddled on them."

One captain asked how Volarin could be so sure that Spurgle had actually escaped. Volarin flicked a switch on his wrist PDA. A new video was shown on the projection hovering over his arm. The angle was from the upper corner of the emergency access hallway. It showed Spurgle bashing at the panel with a fire extinguisher, trying to access an escape shuttle with a group of waiting Spurgleites. Somehow, in all his percussive panic, he hit the right button on the screen, gaining access to the shuttle.

He then got in, holding up his hand for his people to stay back. He mouthed some words that weren't picked up on the tape, before turning back to the interior panel of the shuttle doors and slapping another "device" onto it. The tiny little thing sparked, then arced electricity through the area, frying the door controls and initiating the shuttle's emergency launch sequence. The shocked expression on Spurgle's face was only exceeded by the stunned looks on the faces of his erstwhile followers as the doors slid shut, locking them out of escape. Then it launched, sucking multiple followers out of the ship to cartwheel out into the black.

"If that isn't clear enough, I confirmed the ship was missing one of its escape shuttles. While we were moving to capture him, the Federation took us by surprise, hence the loss of ships. I also lost a marine in the spray explosion. I got out of there in my flagship, but only barely.

"Once we escaped the heat from the Federation, I followed the fuel trails from the shuttles through the sector we had found him in. They all led to one of two separate planets. Spurgle could have landed on either."

Volarin pushed a different button on his PDA. Replacing the CCTV footage of the hallway in the derelict, a small sector map appeared, tracing the celestial bodies in their current region of space. This gave a full three-dimensional map of the various orbits in reference to each other and their current positions. There were three stars in the sector where Spurgle's ship had been found: two yellows and a red. Each one of those stars had planets in orbit. Two dots began to shine as they looped around two of the stars. Small information packets appeared in the hologram. Krokun leaned forward and reached out to poke one.

The information appeared from the prompt, scrawled across the screen for the two celestial bodies and their potential inhabitants. Conversation amongst the others began immediately, but Volarin heard none of it. He had already memorized the information. He was busy once again watching the reactions of the other captains.

Despite this being the first solid lead they had gotten in weeks, everyone looked dejected, or what passed for that emotion amongst their particular intergalactic species. It was obvious the truth of their situation was weighing them all down.

Space was huge. Flight paths were tricky to track, even in the best of circumstances. Just because Volarin had found trails didn't mean they were for sure Spurgle's trails. They could be from a ship that flew a similar pattern, or had a similar engine. Maybe the instruments had just picked it up. In reality, the bastard could be anywhere. He could be dead! But Andrew Spurgle was what the Defilers needed. If they could claim his bounty, through an intermediary, of course, the Defilers might still live on. The damage he had done might still be repaired.

All of this was a complete fiasco. From the moment they had found him to the collective decision to listen to the fool, Andrew Spurgle had been a blight on their organization. All because he was supposed to be some great saboteur. One hundred million credits—the bill for the damages for his sabotage of Arco Station—had ensured all of the Defilers were practically chomping at the bit to stick him in a uniform, if only for the propaganda alone! The plan had always been to turn him in *eventually*. Now it was all for naught. The videos they had shot and disseminated across the wide bands of the sector had only painted them as collaborators to Spurgle, "The Great Liberator." More like the idiot savant. Federation ships hunted them worse than they ever had. The Defilers had lost their reputation for competence, their name no longer driving fear into government officials across the stars.

Volarin still did not understand how his people had been so thoroughly taken in by the man. It was like he had some sort of "idiot" charm to him. All of the Defilers who had spoken with him directly had felt it, once their translators had sorted out his grunting language. Spurgle was oddly magnetic, like watching a boulder rolling downhill or glimpses of a supernova beginning. It might destroy something, it might not; watching the near misses was just as thrilling.

The other captains had settled into arguing over where to send ships when the door banged open once again to reveal another of their number. That made seven of them here so far. This captain was a skinny Zoarc. Her fins swished back and forth as she described finding nothing in her assigned search zone. At the additional bad news, all the captains settled into a meal brought out by a Defiler on standby. No one even made eye contact, let alone spoke.

That little state of affairs lasted only one more hour before the eighth captain arrived. Lorpo strolled into the room, his usual smug expression gone. It was instead replaced by a deep frown. Lorpo got to the table, doubled back for a bottle of depressant, then returned and spoke.

"The high stakes card game was a complete bust." This time the chorus was more yelling than groans. Lorpo had their six hands in the air, held up like a bulwark against the sounds of disappointment and metaphorical, and occasionally literal, sounds of knuckles cracking.

"It's not my fault! I knew the idiot didn't know how to play Shav-vahs, even if he did get the greeting down correctly. Only the gods of the great green sea knew how he learned that."

The story continued, more groans echoing out into the space as it did. Volarin listened intently while watching the others for signs of violence.

He was surprised, though. Maybe Spurgle had a Cuacti follower, and so learned their great game. Shav-vahs was a Cuacti card game filled with asinine rituals, one of which was where you said your family name, your given name, then your family name again when greeting a new player. It was an odd custom only found amongst the Cuacti people that made its way into their favorite game. Evidently, the idiot savant had managed to drunkenly mumble "Spurgle, Andrew Spurgle" at the dealer, then at each player, sometimes repeatedly, whenever he was asked a question or otherwise prompted during play.

"I had hoped that his backers would realize he was a phony, especially when he came in that ridiculous flashy outfit he had found, that 'Tucks-Edo' or whatever, but they didn't, despite my attempts to surreptitiously inform them. His rep as a 'saboteur extraordinaire' meant everyone thought he was bluffing when all he was doing was betting at random." The last line came out in a tone that made it sound like Lorpo had eaten mud. He despised the words coming from his mouth, likely more than anyone else in the room. Save maybe one.

Krokun grunted. "Well, what about you? You're supposed to be the best player in the Defilers! What about the money we staked to get you in?"

"I didn't exactly lose it. The casino just won't release it." Lorpo took a step back as the room exploded in yells of fury. "Look, when it came to the card game, I was fine; someone should have said he was an expert fighter and sent me some proper backup!"

Fendaliss made eye contact with Volarin. He could tell they were both thinking it. Volarin bit the plasma round and asked. "Lorpo, Spurgle is an *awful* fighter. We couldn't teach him anything. He couldn't even handle a plasma pistol, and those things have no recoil."

"He met a master or something and has been training. He was using some sort of combat art, at least a portion of it." When no one else interrupted, he huffed for a moment before coming back to the table. "Anyway, it came down to just me, a very good Kajian, and Spurgle in the final round somehow. The idiot was drinking heavily. He took a shot of Lagar juice meant for the Kajian, thinking it was something called a 'shaken' martini, whatever that is. Then he passed out. He was taken to his room and the game was supposed to start again the next day."

For once, the room was silent, everyone waiting with bated breath for the story to conclude.

"I wasn't about to let the idiot have even that chance, so I broke into his room. Little did I know, like I mentioned, he's a skilled combatant. Maybe he just studied my people. I guess it explains how he knew the Cuacti Shav-vahs greeting." Lopro gestured to a crease near one of his many armpits. "It's not well-known that hitting us here will disable the arm for a time. He kept yelling out the words 'judo chop' as he struck me with the flat edge of his appendage during our fight while he aimed for the joints of my body. It was the only blow he used, almost like I was beneath any other fighting styles. Before long, he was out of the room, and I was left half-paralyzed on the ground to be picked up by hotel security. It took all my remaining money to bribe them into releasing me with a promise to show up for the casino's inquiry."

Lorpo had by then drained the last of the depressant in the bottle and began stumbling over to the crate on the side of the room that Volarin had grabbed from before.

"Otherwise, that's all I have. My ship and crew have no clue where he might be." The Cuacti shrugged and returned to the table, the new bottle turned up and rapidly draining.

The arguing started up the moment he stopped speaking. Once again, the only thing that stopped it was the sounds of another captain arriving.

Elhamora stalked in, her thin and pointed insectile face hard to read. If you didn't know Prokonian physiology, you might have guessed she was angry. That, combined with the spectacle of a Prokonian covered in what looked like coloured dust—painting her chitinous shell like a rainbow—made discerning her mood fairly difficult.

The key thing with their species was the wings. They fluttered so fast as to be only partially visible. It was a clear sign of excitement to anyone who had interacted with the insectile species. That level of vibration was bordering on giddiness.

When the rest of the captains said nothing, tension in the air, Elhamora quietly slid her wrist PDA down on the table. Volarin noted how shoddy it looked and picked it up. Quickly, he brought up the hologram projector to view the recording and slid the device into the center of the table for better viewing.

It showed the perspective of Elhamora's second-in-command, for some reason. The captain was visible on the feed, her team pushing their way through a festival, crowds packed tight into the streets of the city they were in. Federation civilians were celebrating something only the planet likely knew, by hurling huge clumps of coloured dust onto each other. The stuff apparently had mild hallucinogenic properties to it, which made all the festival goers giddy. It all looked rather fun unless you knew the stakes of the captain's search.

The feed continued, showing Elhamora and her team as they stalked around the streets in search of their quarry. The video suddenly got shaky as Elhamora's second evidently began running. In a flash of movement on the feed, everyone else in the room knew why.

In the corner of the frame, Andrew Spurgle could be seen, naked, coated in multiple gaudy colors yet somehow still *shiny*, while being carried around on a litter by a crowd of the cityfolk.

Elhamora could be seen taking off in front of her second-in-command, flying over the crowds, and all sense of stealth gone. The Prokonian sent a salvo of shots at Spurgle, striking his litter-bearers and starting a panic. Spurgle could be seen jumping to his feet when the shots began pouring in, before trying to run, seemingly remembering he was being held six feet in the air on a litter before he plummeted into the crowd and disappeared.

The chitinous warrior and her crew were visible on the projection diving and dodging, swooping down over the crowd whenever Spurgle came into view through the milling and panicking masses of people. One of the Defilers ran into a huge pane of glass being carried between two workers, shattering it and drawing the ire of said workers and those around them affected by the falling fragments. The Defiler in question could be seen disappearing under a tornado of flailing limbs from the two furious locals and growing crowd. Another Defiler smashed into a cart filled with fruit and coloured dust canisters while diving to grab Spurgle's arm as he stopped to haggle over a morsel, creating a delicious cloud of colored confusion that Spurgle then managed to escape in. The fact he was covered in some sort of grease seemed to be making grabbing him next to impossible.

Even over the chaos of the recording and the people in it, the screams of rage of the crew chasing Spurgle could be heard.

The feed never stopped, revealing that Elhamora had been forced to dip and dodge even more when the festival goers realized she and her crew were after their "guest of honor" and rose in defense of Spurgle. They began hurling their colored dust balls at the Prokonians and her delicate wings. Luckily for Elhamora, she was fast and agile. The feed showed her dropping into the pile of people, and flying out with a few wounds but a wriggling Andrew Spurgle in her grasp. It wasn't long before that state changed.

Elhamora had gotten maybe thirty feet away from the crowd before Spurgle wriggled enough to slip from her hands, falling twenty feet into another roiling mass of angry Federation citizens. It was at this point the bug captain spoke.

Elhamora rubbed her limbs together, making hand signs and vibrating her chitinous plates. The other captains waited until their translators picked through her statement, while they themselves tried to work out her hand signals.

"At first, I thought the mission failed after he dropped into the press of bodies. We had riled them up so badly there was little chance of finding him again. The cityfolk were set on getting to us, as they were quite unhappy with our actions." Wings fluttered, vibrations syncing with the sounds from her chitinous plates. "I assumed the mission to be a complete failure. That was until I realized he had stolen my wrist PDA in our struggle."

Volarin just now realized she wasn't wearing a PDA. Elhamora gestured to the device Volarin was holding, indicating with signs he should search for location data. While he did that, Elhamora continued with her explanation. "It was at this time I contacted a Defiler captain nearby and told them to track my device. The call was answered, and our quarry cornered." Her wings continued fluttering, filling the room with a low buzz.

Volarin flipped through the network until he found what he was looking for. The location data listed her wrist PDA as being only fifty feet away! Volarin began to speak, but was cut off by a figure emerging from the passage into the basement. Elhamora spoke again.

"Xic-xic will finish our shared report."

The tenth captain to arrive came into view. Xic-xic floated into the area, the parts of their body not currently in real space passing through the table and the chair as they "sat down." The pieces were diaphanous to anyone who couldn't see both real and *flux* space at once. Of all the Federation species, Kajians were the strangest.

Part energy, part flesh, Kajians existed partially in the *flux* and partially in real space, making them exceptional pilots and navigators. The voice of Xic-xic filled the back of Volarin's head, even and unsettling for the lack of a physical cue from the captain.

"*I SEE MANY I EXPECTED, YET NOT ALL. WE ARE MISSING COICAR?*" Xic-xic turned to Volarin as they said it. The volume in Volarin's head seemed to turn up as they did. He would never truly get used to it.

Fendaliss waved a tired hand. "They have yet to return with their reports."

The Kajian shifted their visage to take in the room. The words they used felt like they were coated in acid, for how they settled into Volarin's brain. They filled his cranium, cutting into his psyche, while seeming to echo like a deep cavern.

"SAD. AN INCOMPLETE GROUPING IS NOT PREFERRED. REGARDLESS, TIME IS OF THE ESSENCE."

Xic-xic's diaphanous form flashed, indicating they were interacting with another energy being far away, likely another Kajian Defiler crewmember on their ship. Time needed to pass for the information to travel between points in the flux. As they spoke with their counterpart, the part of them still in real space launched into their apparent victory speech.

"MY SHIP AND CREW HAD BEEN TRAVELING THROUGH THE PROKONIAN'S ASSIGNED SECTOR FOLLOWING A LEAD, PURELY BY CHANCE. THE CALL CAME THROUGH REGARDING THE PDA AND WE DIVERTED TO ASSIST. WE ARE GLAD WE DID, YET SAD ABOUT THE STATE SPURGLE ENDED UP IN."

The voice abruptly cut out, and Volarin was able to uncross his eyes. Movement near the front door shifted Volarin's view from the energy being to another Kajian and a small retinue following behind.

They came in slowly, at the pace of the awkward burden they were bearing, which was pushed via hovercart into the space where they sat. Once the cart came to a stop, the two Defilers pushing it left the room.

The figure that was carted in was very much dead. They were a bipedal flesh-based sentient. They had peach-pink skin and visible body hair, at least what wasn't thoroughly crisped. They had the same two manipulator appendages that all humans possessed, or at least what used to be appendages. Both ended in a burned and scarred stump.

The face was so heavily charred Volarin couldn't tell if it was Spurgle—there was too much scarring. Had the Kajian lit him on fire? Elhamora stepped forward and began to gesture, beginning to speak, but was interrupted by an enraged Omnikan.

"You blew him up! How can we even confirm it's him?" Krokun was reaching for his plasma pistol again, hand grabbing nothing but the air near his belt.

Volarin looked at the body. Something on its arm glinted in the overhead lights. He pressed a button on his PDA to ping Elhamora's PDA. The device, partially hidden under charred flesh on the arm, pinged back. Volarin pointed to the machine. "Seems good enough for me, Krokun, but the captain is correct: how can you be so sure? Start from the beginning. How did this happen, Xic-xic?" Something was odd, though. Shouldn't the metal be more singed?

"CONFIRMATION OF HIS IDENTITY COMES FROM THE DEVICE. NO ONE BUT A DEFILER CAPTAIN HAS OUR CODES.

"REGARDLESS, I WAS THERE WHEN THE FOOL KILLED HIMSELF—I SAW THE EXPLOSION. IT IS SAD THAT WE CANNOT COLLECT THE LIVING BOUNTY, BUT A DEAD MAN CAN STILL HAVE HIS NEURAL PATHWAYS READ. THE EVIDENCE CAN STILL BE PRODUCED."

Volarin sighed. "That doesn't always work on the fleshier species Xic-Xic."

The Kajian turned to view him. *"IT DOES NOT?"* Volarin shook his head. For once, the quasi-*flux* creature looked at a loss. The energy field that made up their body began to shrink and sputter, like a lamplight running out of oil. Elhamora buzzed again, translator speaking for her.

"And what did you all do? At least we captured the threat to our very existence. Listen to the retelling before you discount the results."

Seemingly mollified that they were out of the direct scrutiny of so many angry terrorists for even a moment, Xic-xic began to glow brightly again. They launched back into their story.

"SPURGLE HAD FOUND A WAY TO ESCAPE ELHAMORA, BUT COULD NOT LEAVE THE PLANET HE WAS ON. WE FOUND HIM SITTING AND WATCHING ANOTHER FESTIVAL ON THE OPPOSITE SIDE OF THE WORLD FROM THE PROKONIAN CAPTAIN WITH AN HONOR GUARD OF FEDERATION MILITIA.

"THE FESTIVAL WAS SOME SORT OF GATHERING WHERE LOCALS TIED COLORFUL EXPLOSIVES TO WEAPONS AND HIT EACH OTHER WITH THEM IN MOCK COMBAT. ONE STRIKE MEANT YOU WERE OUT. WHAT FUN, CORRECT?

"IT TOOK LITTLE CONVINCING AND ONLY A FEW CREDITS TO GAIN ENTRY, THEN LITTLE EFFORT TO CHALLENGE SPURGLE. THE FOOL SHOWED UP TO BATTLE MY UNDERLING WITH A CUSTOM-MADE WEAPON HE HAD ADJUSTED HIMSELF. SADLY, WE FAILED TO NOTICE THE MODIFICATION UNTIL IT WAS TOO LATE.

"MY UNDERLING DODGED ALL HIS FEEBLE BLOWS, TAUNTING SPURGLE ABOUT THE PDA AND HIS STUPIDITY. THAT WAS, UNTIL THE CROWD GOT ANGRY AT THEIR 'HERO' LOSING. PEOPLE BEGAN TO RUSH THE COMBAT FIELD, FORCING MY UNDERLING INTO A PRECARIOUS POSITION. I MENTALLY INSTRUCTED THEM TO TAKE A BLOW FROM SPURGLE BEFORE SIGNALING THE FLAGSHIP AND GRABBING HIM. WINNING WAS NOT THE OBJECTIVE. THIS, IN RETROSPECT, WAS A MISTAKE.

"SPURGLE HAD STRAPPED SO MANY EXPLOSIVES TO HIS WEAPON, IT WENT FROM BEING A PRETTY LIGHT SHOW ON CONTACT INTO AN ACTUAL BOMB."

All the heads in the room turned to regard the charred form of Andrew Spurgle lying on the cart. They all knew how the story would end. Even Krokun stayed silent.

"MY UNDERLING WENT TO GRAB HIM WHILE TAKING THE BLOW ON HIS CHEST. THIS ENTANGLED THEM FOR THE ENSUING EXPLOSION, WHICH SENT THEM AND SEVERAL OTHERS CLOSE BY THIRTY FEET INTO THE AIR, SPINNING AWAY TOGETHER TO LAND IN A SMOKING HEAP AMONGST THE CROWD. WHEN WE REACHED THEM AND GOT THE CROWD AWAY, WE TOOK NO CHANCES. WE GRABBED THE BODY WITH THE PDA AND LEFT."

The captains all looked at each other, then back at the corpse. Weeks of searching. Hundreds of their people had died. Despite it ending with a bang for Xic-xic, this felt more like a whimper to Volarin.

Lorpo was the first to speak up. "So, that's it, then?"

As reality came crashing down on them all, the collective mood lightened considerably.

The captains began hooting and hollering, congratulating the two successful captains on their hard work. Xic-xic glowed brightly and Elhamora buzzed in place. Volarin went to join them before he heard two plasma rounds going off above him on the main floor. He shouted for silence, which came only after much cajoling.

Many pairs of boots were slowly walking across the floor. Every captain in the room turned to follow the sound while hands grabbed at belts for weapons that were sitting upstairs with the doorman. They waited until the boots faded, then the sounds of several people descending the ladder and approaching the open doorway. Captains began to fan out, flipping over chairs and trying to find cover in the open, hard-to-defend room.

Two figures walked into the light, both standing in battle suits. Behind them were more suited figures, all holding very nice-looking plasma rifles.

One of the battle-suited figures stepped forward. The visor on the helmet dropped down, revealing a face Volarin had been seeing in his dreams.

Instead of lying on the hovercart, burnt to a crisp like he was supposed to be, the smiling, smug face of Andrew Spurgle could be seen surveying the room. His beady eyes swept across the table and the occupants until they had taken in the full space. He stepped forward one more pace, pulling out two plasma pistols and holding them akimbo. Behind him, the other battle-suited figure took out a pair of handcuffs. Spurgle then launched into his own victory speech.

"You came close, but you can't scam Andrew Spurgle! I've known sleight of hand since I was five, so swapping that smart watch that guy kept talking about was a breeze!" He pointed to Xic-xic. "Your man made a wonderful pillow upon landing, by the way." He smiled again. Volarin had trouble not leaping over the table. "You almost got me on whatever that planet was called, then on that other planet, too, the one with the aliens! But I have eyes in every system, alie— I mean, *people*, good people, just the best people, in every sector! One message on my network got me new allies. Say hello to the Bombora Despoilers, my new organization for fighting the Federation! No matter what you try, you can't stop the great spy Andrew Spur—" The other figure stepped forward and slapped the cuffs on Spurgle midsentence while jamming an EMP disc onto the back of his suit. Volarin watched as Andrew Spurgle was quickly rendered a shaking, whimpering, electrified mess on the floor.

The figure stepped over him, but didn't lower their visor like Spurgle had. They only glanced at the man once, and then only to shake their head in what Volarin assumed was disgust. Instead, they stretched out their arm and activated the projection screen on the suit's built-in PDA. The face and upper torso of a standard looking intergalactic citizen was visible, wearing a beautiful, well-cut gray uniform. Directly next to the face was the flashing emblem of the Federation Secret Police.

"Thank you, Mr. Spurgle. Couldn't have done it without you. Sorry for the flashy entrance, folks. I'm Special Agent Vitalar Corso, at your service. Oh, and you are all under arrest."

The Last Flight of Samson, the Giant Fiberglass Bull

Ted Begley

It was a quiet Sunday afternoon in late August when Judge Joseph Flynn drove back into town from a weeklong fishing trip with his son-in-law, Dan Rogers, the local District Attorney, and Clarence Simon, the town's Chief of Police. Clarence had a rustic cabin on a lake about two hours away from Midvale, and the three men had spent their time there swapping stories, catching, cleaning, and packing fish, and generally relaxing. The judge had a cooler full of walleye in the back of his car and was looking forward to having a few of them for dinner with his family before going back to his usual routine the next morning.

The judge had just dropped off his son-in-law and was making his way around the block to his own home where his wife, Suzanne, and their only child, Amanda, were waiting. After Dan had a chance to clean up and change, he was going to join the family at the judge's house and have a nice Sunday dinner before taking Amanda and their six-year-old daughter, Katie, home. Amanda—Mandy to the judge—had temporarily moved back into the family home for the past week to keep her mother company while the men bonded. It also gave the judge's wife an opportunity to dote on her granddaughter. The thought of the family all being together put the judge in a very serene state.

His serenity was abruptly shattered as soon as he turned the corner onto his street and saw a twenty-foot-long fiberglass bull protruding awkwardly from the roof of his home.

Judge Flynn pulled up to the curb across the street from his house, a pale yellow, two-story Cape Cod with green shutters and a tree-lined lawn, mostly because the Midvale Fire Department ladder truck was occupying his driveway. He turned off the engine, got out of his car, and surveyed the scene. Besides the giant black fiberglass bull on the roof, there appeared to be about twenty-five to thirty people standing on his front lawn looking up at the spectacle. His wife and daughter were there, as well as most of the Fire Department, a smattering of neighbors, and Pete Winslow, a junior at the local college who was the captain of the Academic Knowledge team. Judge Flynn approached the group while doing his utmost to remain calm.

Pete was the first person to notice the judge heading their way. While not imposing in stature—Judge Flynn was only five and a half feet tall and wore old-fashioned, horn-rimmed glasses—he was definitely imposing in his presence of personality, despite the high-pitched squeak that occasionally came out when he was flustered.

Pete decided that the judge looked flustered.

The judge was marching in a straight line to where his wife was standing. Pete moved to join them because, to his regret, he could probably offer the judge at least a partial explanation of events. Pete managed to get to the family at the same moment as the judge.

"Good afternoon, Your Honor," Pete said, just as the judge opened his mouth to speak.

"Afternoon, Pete," the judge replied, purposefully omitting the "good," given the presence of the fiberglass monstrosity lodged firmly in the attic above Suzanne Flynn's second-floor craft room. The judge turned to his wife and daughter and asked, "Is everyone okay? Where's Katie?"

"We're all fine, dear," Suzanne told her husband. "Katie is next door, playing board games with the Lawson children." Judge Flynn breathed a sigh of relief. "You don't need to worry, dear—no one was in the house when our visitor dropped in. Amanda and I were out at the market, buying some last-minute groceries for dinner." Suzanne Flynn smiled at her husband and softly patted his cheek.

"Well, that's a relief. But how did *that* happen?" the judge asked, pointing up at the fiberglass bull.

Before his wife could answer, a loud voice from above called out, "Good afternoon, Judge Flynn!" All eyes returned upward, where, now that he was in a better position, the judge could see Andrew Spurgle dangling upside down from the neck of the bull, tethered by a rope tangled around his skinny legs. If it were possible, the judge was even more shocked and surprised. All he could do was wave at Andrew and nod.

After a moment or two to collect himself, the judge took a deep breath and in a forced calm voice, said, "I can see what happened," he began, glancing at Andrew, "but can someone please explain to me *how* it happened?"

"I think I can explain what happened, Your Honor," Pete said meekly.

Judge Flynn turned to face Pete directly, and with his voice slightly raised, asked, "Pete, did you have something to do with this?" The judge ended his question with an involuntary squeak on the last syllable.

Pete winced slightly at the question and replied, "Well...not intentionally. I was trying to help Andrew figure out an easy way to move the bull and run interference for any really bad ideas that he was bound to come up with. But Andrew started moving the bull before I could get there, and his plan didn't work out so well."

"That, my dear boy, is an understatement," the judge said, his eyes returning to the figure of Andrew, literally twisting in the wind. The judge removed his glasses and began to absently clean them. His wife and daughter moved to either side of him to offer a comforting hug. Once his family had embraced him, Judge Flynn patted his wife's hand and put his glasses back on. He looked up at Andrew again, then back to Pete.

"Okay, Pete," the judge said, somewhat calmer, "why don't you fill me in on what you know about this?"

"Sure thing, Your Honor," Pete said, and gestured towards a picnic table and some chairs that had recently been set up in the front yard. A group of their neighbors were putting out a variety of food for the impromptu gathering. The family made their way to the chairs and Pete began filling them in on the details. "It all started four days ago," Pete began, "when the Conestoga Ranch Steakhouse burned down."

"Wait...what?" the judge exclaimed. "The Conestoga burned down? Poor Fred and Jean. That restaurant has been in their family for three generations."

"Don't worry, sir," Pete said, "nobody was hurt and they have plans to rebuild. Pastor Evans loaned them the revival tent, and they'll be using it for an al fresco dining room until the new building is ready. That's where Andrew comes into the picture. They gave him the restaurant's mascot, Samson."

"That's Samson?" the judge asked, shading his eyes with one hand and squinting up at the bull. "Why on earth would Fred and Jean give Samson away if they plan on rebuilding?"

"If I understand correctly, they plan to buy one of those newer fiberglass bulls with the lighted message board on either side so they can post daily specials and announce events and such," Pete continued. "Samson had been showing signs of his age, too, so they decided it was time to replace him. Andrew was there when they made the decision, and asked Fred if he could have the bull."

"Why on earth would Andrew want a giant bull?" Mrs. Flynn asked Pete as she poured everyone a glass of ice-cold lemonade from a large beverage cooler that had been set out on the table.

Pete took a sip of the lemonade before replying. "Andrew wants to give it to Mr. Martin to put at the entrance to the dairy. He's been awfully nice to Andrew over the years. Andrew was only ten when his father passed away and Mr. Martin was the one who gave Andrew his first job, mucking the barn," he told Mrs. Flynn. Pete thought for a moment and added,

"I think Andrew sees giving him Samson as a way to make up for the problems he's caused Mr. Martin over the years, as well. Andrew's always had more enthusiasm than skill."

"That's a very polite way of saying that Andrew is a bumbler," the judge interjected as he sipped at his lemonade. "But now that we've established the who and why, the question of how still remains."

"The next morning, after the fire, Andrew went over to help the Simons clean up the fire debris," Pete said, continuing the timeline of events. "There were a bunch of students from the college there, too, including me. At one time or another, quite a few of us local students have made a little extra money working for Mr. and Mrs. Simon, at special events if not as regular employees. We were all doing what we could to give back in their time of need."

"That was very sweet of all of you," Mrs. Flynn told Pete. "We have such civic-minded students at Midvale College."

"Thank you, ma'am," Pete replied, his cheeks becoming somewhat flushed. He cleared his throat and continued. "Andrew noticed that Samson had been moved to the area of debris that was going to be hauled away. He thought it might be a mistake, so he asked Mr. Simon about it, and found out about the replacement bull that he planned to order. That's when Andrew got the idea to give Samson to Mr. Martin as a surprise. Mr. Simon said he was okay with it, but advised Andrew that Samson had to be moved by Monday morning, to be out of the way for the construction crew."

"So how does moving a fiberglass bull by Monday lead it to being stuck in my roof on Sunday?" the judge asked, gesturing towards the house. Without thinking, the small group looked in that general direction, in time to see the firefighters sliding a very long board through the now open gable vent at the end of the attic. The Fire Chief could be heard directing his crew to get the board on top of the joists, under the bull's legs. They were doing their best to stabilize the bull before trying to untangle Andrew.

The group's attention moved back to Pete. "I was helping Mr. Simon at the time of the conversation," Pete resumed, "so when he gave Samson to Andrew, I offered to help him move it. We all know how Andrew gets sometimes, and I hoped that I could redirect any of the more 'imaginative' ideas that he might have. Besides, I felt like I still owed him one for finding the goat last year."

Everyone nodded at the last comment. Just before last year's big intercollegiate academic knowledge championship, a group of sophomores from Springfield College had tried to frame Pete for stealing a goat, their school's mascot, in a misguided effort to keep him from competing. Andrew had been instrumental in finding the goat, even though—being Andrew—he also managed to get all concerned parties covered in peanut butter...including the poor, innocent goat. Andrew had been so gung-ho that he had temporarily forgotten about his own peanut allergy before quite literally rushing headlong into a peanut butter factory. After a trip to the emergency room, all had ended reasonably well.

It was then that Chief Simon arrived. He pulled up in front of the house in his cruiser with the lights on but the siren off. When he got out of the car, he strode across the lawn, passing the judge and the group discussion, and came to stand about ten feet away from the front porch where he could see Andrew, who was still dangling upside down and twisting slightly in the breeze. The chief remained dressed in the clothes he had been wearing at the cabin that very morning, including his fishing vest and hat. When Andrew rotated back around to where he could see Chief Simon, he shouted down, "Hey, Chief! Your brother gave me Samson! Isn't it great? Oh, hey, have you been fishing?"

Chief Simon became somewhat flustered by the nonchalant nature of Andrew's greeting and made a few guttural sounds, sputtering a bit before he could form a coherent response. "Andrew," he finally managed to say, "what in the devil are you doing up there?"

"Sorry, Chief," Andrew shouted back, "I can't quite hear you. My ears are stopped up from hanging here. Pete's over there with the judge. He can tell you everything." And with that, Andrew rotated back to facing the bull.

Chief Simon turned and looked around the yard until he saw the judge and his family sitting with Pete Winslow. The Chief walked over to them and realized that he must have stormed right passed them. When he got to within normal speaking distance, he looked at Pete and asked, "What do you know about this mess?"

Before Pete could answer, Mrs. Flynn asked the chief what *he* knew of the situation. Chief Simon graciously accepted a glass of lemonade, and informed them of several messages which had been on his machine when he got home, including one from his brother about the restaurant fire and subsequent cleanup, one from the city planner about permits to move large objects, and the last message he received, just as he was getting home, was from Tim Hardy, the Flynns' neighbor across the street, informing him that Samson was lodged in the judge's attic, and that someone was hanging upside down from its neck. The common theme in all of the messages was Andrew Spurgle.

At the mention of Tim Hardy's name, the man came across the street dragging his charcoal grill behind him. He was heading toward an area of the judge's front lawn where several more folding tables were being set up. A large spread of food was now on the tables which had been set out previously. It appeared that while Pete was getting the judge up to speed, the small gathering of neighbors was turning into a self-perpetuating block party.

"That pretty much brings you up to the same point we are, Clarence," the judge said, gesturing at a lawn chair for the Chief to sit down. "Now, Pete, if you would be so kind as to explain how Andrew got the bull on my roof?" The judge once again ended his sentence with a high-pitched squeak.

"Yes, sir," Pete said as the Chief pulled up a chair and joined the proceedings. "Andrew crashed Samson into your roof with a balloon."

The judge took off his glasses and rubbed his hand over his face. His wife reached over and gently stroked his back while he was doing this. After a few minutes, the judge put his glasses back on and told Pete, "As with anything Andrew does, I think you had better go back to telling us what happened in chronological order so we can have some kind of grasp of his thought process. What happened after Fred gave Andrew the bull?"

"Andrew told me that he was going to ask around and see if he could borrow something to haul the bull over to the dairy farm," Pete said, continuing with the chain of events. "I thought it would be best to contact someone down at city hall and see if we needed any permits; after all, Samson is rather large."

At the mention of Samsom, everyone looked up at the roof of the house. "I told Ms. Miller at the City Planner's office what Andrew had in mind, and she said that Samson's dimensions were small enough to not need a permit, but she advised us to avoid Main Street with all of the 'Welcome Students' banners that the college had put up. They might be lower than our clearance."

"Janet is always knowledgeable about such things," the judge's daughter, Amanda Rogers, contributed. "You may not have needed a permit, but Janet will almost certainly have pertinent advice."

"She does and she did," Pete said. "Janet suggested that I check with the construction company that is working on rebuilding the Conestoga. One of their bulldozers was brought in on a trailer big enough to accommodate Samson. I spoke with Mr. Ferguson, the crew foreman, and he told me that as soon as they dropped off the second bulldozer on Monday, he'd have his men load Samson up on the trailer and bring the bull to the dairy farm. That apparently wasn't good enough for Andrew. Mr. Simon had said to have Samson out of there by Monday morning, and Andrew thought that was cutting it too close."

"Doesn't that boy pay attention to anything?" the judge asked rhetorically. "He was to have it moved to be out of the way of the construction company. The construction company was the one offering to move it." The judge threw up his arms in exasperation. Mrs. Flynn put her arm across her husband's shoulders in an effort to help calm him.

It was then that they spotted Dan Rogers walk around the house from the direction of the back yard. As he approached the front of the house, he was transfixed by the sight of the bull on the roof. The fire department had just finished putting a second board under the hooves of the bull and had evenly distributed its weight across the joists. Fairly soon, they could begin the process of untangling Andrew without having to worry about the bull shifting on them while they worked. Amanda called out to her husband and waved him over to the smaller gathering under the elm tree, among what had turned into a rather large neighborhood party.

Once Dan joined the group, Amanda brought him up to date on the events that Pete had described so far, and hastily assured him that their daughter was safe at a neighbor's house. When Amanda reached the point where Pete had left off, Dan turned to Pete and asked, "Is all of this," he gestured at the roof, "the reason the back of the house looks like it's covered in Mylar and fishing nets?"

"The back of our house is covered in what!" the judge exclaimed, sharply turning his head to look at Pete. The judge gestured impatiently for Pete to continue.

Pete cleared his throat. "That would be what's left of the balloon that I mentioned earlier." The full attention of the small group was once again focused on Pete. "You see, unknown to me at the time, Andrew had been earning extra money working for the Agricultural Department at Midvale College. He worked in the barn where they study Animal Husbandry, cleaning out the stalls. That's right next to the field where the Science Department runs some of their experiments. Last week while Andrew was at work, one of the professors was out in the field inflating a scientific research balloon—one of those high altitude, long duration balloons. Andrew went over and started chatting with the professor about the balloon when it failed its preflight checks. Something to do with the seams having a defect that could cause a leak. So naturally, Andrew asked if he could have the balloon. I suppose the professor thought he meant for recycling."

"Andrew collects the most unusual variety of things," Mrs. Flynn said. "What do you suppose he does with all that stuff?"

"From the looks of things," Chief Simon said bluntly, "he uses them to leave a wake of mayhem and destruction behind him." It was at that moment the fire department began positioning the aerial on the ladder truck to gain access to Andrew. "Or under him, as the case may be," the Chief added, gesturing towards the roof.

The judge cleared his throat to get the group's attention. "Pete, why don't you tell us what Andrew did with the balloon after he got it?"

"Andrew told me about the balloon yesterday while we were preparing Samson for the move, but I thought it was just idle chit-chat," Pete said, reaching over and helping himself to a tuna salad sandwich from a nearby table. "I didn't think anything about it until I got a call from Deputy Green this morning. He told me he saw Andrew attaching the harness we made to lift Samson onto a trailer to a rather large balloon. Naturally, I got in my car and drove over to the Conestoga as fast as I could. When I got there, Andrew already had the balloon inflated and Samson was about ten feet in the air with two tether lines attached to the rear bumper of Andrew's Jeep. His idea was to slowly drive Samson over to the dairy farm like some sort of Macy's Thanksgiving Day balloon."

"That really is a clever idea," said Amanda.

"If it had been a clever idea," her father retorted, "then there wouldn't be a giant fiberglass bull sticking out of my roof."

The judge hiccupped as he completed the sentence. His wife knew that he must be agitated more than she originally thought if the hiccups were coming on.

The conversation lulled while the judge drank a glass of water to help alleviate the involuntary contractions of his diaphragm. He was just beginning to feel somewhat better when he looked around and noticed there appeared to be about a hundred people gathered on his and the neighbor's lawns, overflowing into the street. The judge saw that Tim Hardy had three grills going now. It was time to find out what was going on.

"Pete, wait here for a minute," Judge Flynn stated. "I want to hear the rest of this story, but I need to talk to Tim first."

The judge walked across his lawn to where Tim was grilling and asked him, with that squeak returning to his voice, "Tim, why on God's green earth has half the neighborhood gathered at my house for a Sunday picnic?"

Tim looked up from his cooking and smiled. "Come on, Joe, you've got to be kidding. This is the best show in town right now. It's not often you get to witness an Andrew Spurgle stunt in action. Besides, if you haven't noticed, Andrew's balloon is draped over the power lines, so the fire department had to cut the electricity to the street, which means this is the only game in town. And if anyone is going to eat right now, it's either cold cuts or grilling out. Don't worry, I'm sure you'll feel better after you've had something to eat."

The judge waved in resignation and said, "Fine, just keep everyone at a safe distance from the house."

"Sure thing, Joe," Tim replied. "By the way, we're running out of hamburgers, hotdogs, and brats. You wouldn't have anything to contribute to the cookout, would you?" Tim asked with an expectant grin.

The judge sighed and said, "Sure, Tim. There's a large cooler of walleye fillets in the back of my station wagon. Help yourself."

"Thanks, Joe," Tim said heading toward the vehicle. "I'll have you and the family a fish dinner ready before you know it."

The judge went back over to join his wife and tell her about the power outage and how the neighbors were using the minor inconvenience as an opportunity for the gathering. Chief Simon radioed his officers to set up barricades at each end of the block and to join the crowd once they were done. Having taken care of the immediate concerns, they once again turned their attention back to Pete so he could finish telling them about Andrew's misadventures.

"Let's get back to Andrew now, Pete," the judge said as he and the Chief both settled back into their respective lawn chairs. "Before the interruption, Andrew had Samson airborne and tied to the back of his Jeep. What happened next?"

"Well, Judge," Pete said, "I asked Andrew what he thought he was doing, and he told me that he got the idea from watching all of those holiday parades with the massive balloons. He was going to slowly tow Samson over to Martin's Dairy Farm. He claimed to have inflated the balloon only enough to get Samson buoyant. I checked and Samson wasn't really pulling taut against the ropes, just floating about ten feet up. That's when Andrew asked me to help guide Samson over. I knew if I didn't help, he would just do it on his own and probably get into trouble."

"He succeeded in getting in trouble, anyway," the judge said, looking up as the fire department began cutting Andrew loose. Two firefighters had Andrew's head and shoulders elevated as a third one began cutting the ropes around his waist and legs. It would only be a few more minutes before they had him down.

"Yes, he did," Pete agreed. "But, at first, it looked like Andrew's idea was working. I insisted on driving, thinking that would be where any issues would arise, and Andrew sat in the back, keeping an eye on Samson and the tether lines. Andrew had scouted out the best route yesterday and I agreed. We started our trip away from the Conestoga on the old farm to market road that loops to the west of town. There are no overhead power or phone lines there, and it's a level road, more or less."

"That would be the best choice of route," Chief Simon agreed. "Very few trees along that road too."

"Not few enough," Pete sighed. "We were about halfway to the dairy when we approached a grove of walnut trees on the edge of the Granby farm. Some of the limbs hang out over the road, at the curve. It's a popular place for bicyclists to pull off and rest in the shade. Sadly, it's not the best place to pass if you're towing a balloon with a large bull attached. We couldn't find a good way to get around the trees without snagging the tow lines. Andrew finally decided to tie a third rope around Samson and pull him sideways, towards the opposite side of the road. It almost worked, too, but the netting around the balloon caught on one of the taller walnut tree limbs."

"It's a wonder that the limb didn't puncture the balloon," Dan observed.

"Not immediately, anyway," Pete said, "but it was the beginning of the end for the balloon."

"Oh, dear," Mrs. Flynn said as she stood up and refilled her glass of lemonade. "Poor Andrew tries so hard. If he only had more guidance, he might not get into such precarious situations."

"Andrew decided that he should climb the netting and cut the balloon free. I wasn't too keen on the idea, but he was adamant, so I insisted that he let me tie a rope around his waist and then he could attach it to the netting while cutting the branches free. As he was trimming the last branch back, the balloon shifted in a gust of wind, and a branch poked the defective seam, starting a slow leak. Andrew had a roll of duct tape on him, and he put a piece over the leak. By this time, Samson was barely a foot off the ground. What happened next was rather...unexpected."

"You sort of have to expect the unexpected where it comes to Andrew," Amanda said. "He has a talent for going off on previously unknown tangents."

"That's true," Pete agreed with a slight smile. "Anyway, as Andrew was climbing down, he reached over and opened the valve to the helium tank at the base of the balloon. I suppose he was trying to get Samson higher off the ground. I don't know if maybe he turned the valve too much, or if it was just broken. Either way, the balloon inflated too rapidly, and the tethers became extremely taut, so much so that the balloon pulled the knots free that were holding the ropes to the Jeep's rear bumper."

"Four years in my scout troop," the judge interjected with an exasperated sigh. "I never could teach Andrew enough about knots to get his merit badge."

"The next thing I know," Pete continued, "the balloon was lifting away from the Jeep and Andrew was trying to climb on top of Samson. The last I saw of him, before he drifted out of sight, Andrew had gotten on Samson's back but slid off the other side with his legs tangled up in the tether ropes, hanging upside down under Samson's head."

"Oh, my," said Mrs. Flynn. "Andrew must have been so frightened. I'm glad you made him secure himself, at least. He could have been seriously injured if he had fallen off."

"He may still be seriously injured," muttered the judge while looking sadly at the holes in his roof.

"The only thing I could think of to do," Pete resumed, "was get in the Jeep and follow him. That proved to be more difficult than it sounds. The balloon drifted off in the direction of town, over the Granby farm, and there wasn't a direct road that I could take. I ended up zigzagging around the backroads for miles before I finally caught up with Andrew and the bull over Main Street. The balloon was about a hundred and fifty feet up, and moving east at about five miles per hour. I decided to stop at the firehouse and ask for help."

"That's the first really sensible thing I've heard so far," Chief Simon grumped.

"Be nice," Amanda scolded. "No one can predict which direction Andrew will take off. Especially when the direction is up."

"When I went into the firehouse," Pete continued, "they didn't believe me at first…until I mentioned Andrew's name. Chief Wynn said, 'Why didn't you say that in the first place?' The next thing I know, we're following Andrew in the ladder truck. We had just passed the intersection of Sycamore when I noticed that the temporary duct tape patch was peeling off the damaged seam. A short time later, the bull finally came to rest on your house, and when the balloon deflated to the point that it wasn't holding any of the weight, the legs of the bull went through the roof. The rest you already know. No one was home when it happened. Mrs. Flynn and Amanda came home just a few minutes later, and you showed up about ten minutes after that."

As Pete finished catching them up, their attention returned to the roof, where a now-freed Andrew was being lowered down the ladder, tied into a Stokes basket. The paramedics were waiting on the ground to receive Andrew, but he looked relatively cheerful and none the worse for wear. After he made it to the lawn, he was taken to the ambulance to be checked out. In the meantime, the fire crew on the roof began cutting the balloon away so they could remove it from the power lines and restore electricity to the neighborhood.

Tim Hardy walked up to the little group, carrying a platter of grilled fish. He put the platter down on a nearby table and pulled up a chair to join them. "Well, Joe," he said, leaning back in the chair, "this is turning into the best neighborhood picnic that we've had in years. Andrew really puts on quite a show when he gets focused on a project."

"You may be enjoying all of this, Tim," the judge said, clearly annoyed, "but you're not the one who has holes in his roof."

"Relax, Joe," Tim said with a smile, "you're covered. I sold you your homeowners' policy. Andrew certainly falls under 'Act of God' as part of your comprehensive coverage. Before you got home, I called Kevin Anderson, and he's on his way over with the big crane to lift Samson off the roof. He'll tarp over the holes this afternoon and his crew will be back in the morning to do the repairs. It'll be like it never happened by this time tomorrow. He groused about coming over today, but I told him to bring the family and we would feed them. Their power has been out, too."

"You're a very good friend and neighbor, Tim," the judge said, getting up from his chair. "I probably don't say it enough. I suppose I should go over and talk with Andrew now."

Tim stood up. "I'll go with you. Moral support and such."

The two men walked to the back of the ambulance, where the paramedics were finishing up with Andrew. Except for a couple of rips in his shirt and a bandage on his forehead, he looked perfectly fine. The closest paramedic turned to the judge and stated, "He's got minor scrapes and bruises, but otherwise checks out good."

The paramedic turned to Andrew. "Go see Doctor Gibbons tomorrow and get a thorough physical, just to be on the safe side. If you have any blurred vision or vomiting, go to the emergency room immediately. Otherwise, you're cleared to go home, if you want."

"Thanks," Andrew told the paramedic, then turned to the judge. "Am I in a lot of trouble?" he asked sheepishly.

"Would you listen to that, Tim? 'Am I in a lot of trouble,' he asks. You crashed a giant fiberglass bull into the roof of my house, and you want to know how much trouble you're in? You aren't in nearly as much trouble as you would have been in if you had gotten yourself hurt," the judge replied, gently scolding Andrew. "How would I explain that to your mother? Go in the house, wash up, and come join the picnic. You organized it, whether you meant to or not."

Andrew grinned that shy, disarming smile of his and said, "Yes, sir." He strode to the house and ducked through the front door.

"You know, Joe," Tim said, clasping the judge on the shoulder, "I think you're about as close to a father as that boy has." Tim slapped him on the back and added, "He could do worse."

"Gee, thanks, pal," the judge said, but he appreciated the sentiment, anyway. The whole town had a soft spot for Andrew. Everyone looked out for him. He was friendly and big-hearted, regardless of the results of his attempts at "helping" people. It was hard to stay mad at him. "Let's go try some of those fish you grilled."

The two men went to grab some food, along with everyone else. Pete had begun telling them of some other scheme Andrew was planning involving an old ice cream truck. The judge had missed the first part of this story, but apparently Andrew was going to start working part-time for his uncle at the Twin Pines Lodge to earn some extra money. Hopefully, a job interacting with the public might redirect his enthusiasm in a more constructive way.

The Lawsons had brought Katie back over, now that the fire department was done. The last remnants of the balloon had been cut away and the power had been restored. It looked as if half the town was here at this point. People were filling plates, laughing with friends, and taking pictures of Samson perched atop of the judge's house.

Judge Flynn took a moment to reflect. The damage that had been done to his home was temporary. The community of friends who had turned out was lasting.

Andrew emerged from the house and joined the judge and his family. "I'm really sorry about this, Your Honor," Andrew said. "I never meant for anything like this to happen."

"We know you didn't, dear," Mrs. Flynn said, answering for both of them. "Isn't that right, Joe?"

"That's right," the judge said, smiling back at his wife. He turned to Andrew and said, "The insurance is covering everything and I've been told that by tomorrow afternoon, it will be as if none of this will have happened."

"Don't worry, sir," Andrew said, "I'll be back first thing in the morning to move Samson."

In unison, everyone said, "No!"

Then Tim added more gently, "What we mean, Andrew, is everything has already been arranged. Kevin Anderson is going to get Samson off the roof today and deliver him to the Martin Dairy Farm in the morning. Why don't you get yourself a plate of food and we'll watch them move Samson once the crane arrives?"

Andrew moved over to the closest table to get some lunch.

Mrs. Flynn said, "Thank you, Tim."

Everyone settled back into their chairs to have some lunch and await the arrival of the crane. Pete told everyone about his plans to go to grad school after college. Andrew soon joined them and hastily ate while listening to Pete with rapt attention. It was turning into a reasonably good afternoon for the judge. He had wanted to come home and spend time with his family, and he was. He was also getting to spend time with his friends and neighbors, too. Not bad, giant bull notwithstanding. He was actually at peace.

It was then that Andrew stood up and said, "I think I need to go to the emergency room."

"Is there something wrong, dear?" Mrs. Flynn asked with obvious concern.

"This chicken tastes funny, and I'm starting to feel nauseated," Andrew said while cradling his stomach with his arm.

"That's not chicken, Andrew," the judge said. "That's the walleye I caught at the lake."

"Then I definitely need to go to the hospital," Andrew said with a pained expression and slightly green pallor. "I'm allergic to fish."

Andrew Spurgle's Day in Court

Jay Dee

Deputy Sheriff Jim-Bob Carter stopped by his friend Leroy Johnson's house and called him at the front door. "Hey, Leroy!"

Leroy appeared in T-shirt and underwear. "Hey, Jim-Bob! What's up?"

Jim-Bob is uncomfortable as he says, "I gotta deliver a court summons. You're getting sued."

"Is it that shiftless neighbor again? He's tried more stuff. Let's see that."

Leroy opened the summons. "Says here some guy, Andrew Spurgle, is suing me after he tripped over a stump in my back forty. Andrew Spurgle? Spurgle? I know that name. He's the guy the neighbor lets hunt his farm. He keeps jumping the fence on my back forty and hunting my quail.

"Hmm, let's see. He wants $100,000 for injuring his back when he tripped over a stump in my field, and he wants $900,000 for pain and suffering." Leroy looked up from the document. "That explains all the shady characters asking about my insurance coverage."

⸎

The day arrived.

Leroy sauntered into court wearing blue jeans and his best flannel shirt. The bailiff pointed at a seat.

Precisely at the appointed time, the door to the courtroom opened, and Andrew Spurgle's entourage entered. Leading the pack were three partners from Throckmorton, Throckmorton, and Throckmorton, resplendent in their pinstriped Burberry suits and Italian leather briefcases. They were followed by two men dressed in hospital scrubs, presumably to care for the plaintiff and testify about the extent of his injuries.

Finally, Andrew Spurgle made his grand entrance in a wheelchair pushed by a young woman wearing what suspiciously resembled a naughty nurse costume. Andrew was nattily dressed in a full upper body cast, looking like the very soul of infirmity, emitting moans and groans while being wheeled to the plaintiff's table.

The plaintiff's case was opened by Byron Ulysses Theophilis Throckmorton Sr. The plaintiff wanted a bench trial. Leroy agreed.

The morning was spent with Byron Junior describing the accident on that fateful day, using aerial photographs and sketches to describe how Leroy had constructed a veritable minefield designed to injure the plaintiff, Andrew Spurgle.

Byron the Third spent the afternoon interviewing the medical personnel regarding Andrew Spurgle's injuries and prognosis. Murky x-rays were produced. The one doctor proceeded to describe all the injuries displayed by these unintelligible blobs and streaks. The second doctor testified that Andrew's injuries would require expensive ongoing care. Even Andrew's nurse testified; breaking into tears over his grave injuries.

The plaintiff's case was summarized the following morning by Byron Senior, who characterized Leroy as a reprobate of the lowest character, how the community had lost one of their best and brightest when Andrew was injured, and loudly demanded thousands of dollars to make Andrew whole again, and more for his pain and suffering.

When Senior had returned to his chair, the judge looked at Leroy, who had sat poker-faced through all the proceedings.

"Leroy, do you have any questions for the witnesses?"

"No, Your Honor."

"Do you have any evidence that would dispute their allegations?"

"Yes, Your Honor, I do."

"Let's have it."

A sly smile briefly lit Leroy's face. "Your Honor, I have here a survey by a state-certified surveyor, which shows where the property line is. The plaintiff was on my neighbor's property when he was injured."

The judge took the document and solemnly examined it. The survey was properly documented and duly notarized. He then handed the document to the Throckmortons. The Throckmorton trio compared the survey with their charts and sketches. Third silently returned the survey to the judge. The three Throckmortons stood, closed their briefcases and started for the door. Senior fixed his gaze on Andrew and said, "You'll be getting our bill," and then left.

The naughty nurse cried, "What! There's no money!" She dumped Andrew out of the wheelchair and wheeled it out the door.

Andrew made an amazing recovery. He jumped up and ran for the door. "Wait for me! I can explain!"

The courtroom was silent, save for the court recorder filing a nail. The judge looked over his glasses.

"Leroy, it appears that the plaintiff has withdrawn his case."

"So it would appear."

The judge rapped his gavel. "I declare the case had been decided for the defendant. Case closed with prejudice."

Leroy stood to leave, but the judge continued.

"Leroy, you could have stopped this long before it came to trial."

Leroy smiled. "Yes, Your Honor, but if I had done so, he would have come back with some other cock and bull story. This way, he won't be back."

"Is that survey for real?"

Leroy pursed his lips briefly. "That depends on how you measure the property. The survey was performed using the original deed. The date of the first survey is unknown and the magnetic North has drifted considerably since my great-grandpa bought the property. Who knows where the actual property line is? Agreeable people just say it's where the fence is. In this case, though..." He grinned.

∞

There was, of course, little surprise when the neighbor's farm was sold for a pittance at Sheriff's auction the following spring to pay some unspecified debt.

The recorded buyer was one Leroy Johnson.

The author notes that the story is an embellishment of an actual event. Names have been changed to protect the guilty, the innocent, and everyone else, for that matter.

A Clinic in Gaslighting

Moze Howard

When I started my little vendetta, you see, I wasn't actually looking to ruin a man's life. I guess you could say that I was lucky that way.

It all started with an office retreat to Yosemite Valley in the fall of last year. Teams of three were assembled, drawn randomly from a hat, and I was thrilled when the boss, Mr. Wickerman, and I were selected to be on the same team. Our third, Spurgle, a frumpy, dumpy little man of questionable moral fiber and even more questionable hygiene, made me look even better by comparison. It was time to make my impression.

Before I continue, I suppose I should tell you a little bit about the company we all work for: Malortech. It was originally just "Malort Inc.," but it turns out Malort is a brand of liquor, much to the founder's chagrin, so "tech" was added to the end. This was in spite of the company's production consisting entirely of cheap sunglasses and kazoos. Both Spurgle and I worked under Mr. Wickerman, a middle manager with executive ambitions. He had just enough power to move someone up the corporate ladder while still being accessible to the common man.

Me? I'm Andrew McMillan. Spurgle, who I thought was named Spiegel for the first year he "worked" at the company (I've never seen him do much beyond picking his nose), is also named Andrew, which was why, when we became cubicle neighbors, people started calling us both by our last names.

In my case, I became merely "Mack," which I enjoyed immensely, always having wanted a cool nickname. "Return of the Mack," released in the year I was born, 1996, became my unofficial theme song. I made sure enough people heard it playing on my car stereo as I trolled Malortech's parking lot to where they associated it with me. Soon, people were proclaiming "Return of the Mack" when I came into the office. Maybe not the best way to make your reputation in business, but it was, at least, better than brown-nosing.

So we're in the Valley, camping, living off the land between team-building exercises. We caught fish, picked berries, poisoned ourselves, got gut worms, you get the idea. About half the crew went home sick, leaving nine of us, counting the boss, so when it was time for the hike to the cabin, the teams were of three instead of two. The hike, you should know, was a race through the wilderness to a cozy cabin where a serious spread of delicious eats was laid out for us, with lots of liquor (but no Malort), soda, if you're a baby, and probably other substances that would make the occasion more memorable. The slowest team would be fired, or so they'd say. Really, last place just meant a public shaming and dishing up after everyone else had their food, drink, and anything else they wanted from the spread. Though, I will say, a few people were known to get fired if they washed out during the retreat but, hey, that's Corporate America.

When Wickerman's name was called just after mine, I wanted to celebrate, until Spurgle's name was also called. True, I was guaranteed not to be shamed; Wickerman always got to the cabin first, but this also meant having to put up with Spurgle. He was a fairly new addition, moving into Product Development after pasting a kazoo to some of our sunglasses and calling it a "new product." His blue-light blocking shades called "The Bluey Kazooey" sold next to zero units, but it was enough to get him on the team, pitching stupid bullshit. But that's neither here nor there.

Our names were drawn, Sally, Wickerman's receptionist, shot into the air with the starter pistol, then tore off towards the cabin on her ATV. She was the "judge" of the competition, meaning, really, that she thought it was stupid to race, but still wanted to participate in some way. That girl had Wickerman wrapped around her little finger.

Before I continue, you should know that all the stupid stuff you see in the funny pages about office life...they're pretty much true. You don't rise based on merit, not at Malortech, that's for sure; you either sucked up or impressed in some stupid, charismatic way. I went for charisma; hence the nickname and theme song. I think it was working, too. Wickerman had taken me under his wing, soliciting my feedback on this and that product. Ever since I predicted the failure of The Bluey Kazooey, he all but needed my approval before sending a product up to marketing. Because of this, I was sure that, after I helped Wickerman get to the Cabin first this year, he'd recommend me to move up to middle management, right beside him, with my own team in Product Development.

"Okay boys, I'm gonna let you in on a little secret," said the wily, white-haired corporate climber. "While the rest of our crew are crashing through the forest, machetes a-swingin', we three are taking a shortcut."

"Huh? Shortcut?" blurted the idiot Spurgle, chewing his tongue. "You mean cheating?"

"Jesus, Spurgle, it's not cheating," I retorted. "Nothing in the rules says we have to follow the suggested route."

"Mack's right," said the boss. "I drew the map and wrote the rules myself. Pay attention, now: this is how you get ahead. Honestly, I'm not sure why you two aren't writing this down."

"We don't carry pens and paper, boss. Everything's done on phones," said the mental deficient named Spurgle. Honestly, the man would suffocate to death if ever he closed his mouth.

"Which is why I hit 'record' on my phone the second you started talking, boss," I said. Okay, maybe I brown-nose a little. Don't hate the player; hate the game.

"Well done, Mack, bonus points to you." Wickerman punched my arm. "And for the record, I have a little notepad in the pocket next to my concealed pistol. You whippersnappers honestly should get back to the fundamentals. We're out in nature, for God's sake."

Ultimately, it came down to the valley itself. Ever since the government set Yosemite aside for public use, human hands, human tools, and human asses had been all over it. We cut down Wickerman's shortcut, leading to a broad path between two rock walls so sheer I thought that maybe they'd been cut. "Hey, that sign over there says 'Beware: Falling Rocks.' How often do the rocks fall, do you think?"

"Not often, Mack," said Wickerman, "and usually not without provocation. Nobody's striking pitons or hacking away with a climbing pick, so we should be fine. Y'know, unless someone started screaming or something."

"Wow!" screamed Spurgle from my other side. He was staring up at a vein of some blue mineral running through the rock. "Do you think that's turquoise?"

"Dude! We're right here!" I whisper-screamed back. "Pipe down!"

"What?" wailed Spurgle.

"Holy shit. Boy! Shut up and get over here!" shouted the boss, a little too loudly, but apparently not loud enough.

"What?" shouted Spurgle, removing wireless earbuds from his ears. "Oh, sorry about that, I was listening— What's that?"

Rumbling, a cascade of stone fell from overhead and Spurgle stood flat-footed, mouth agape, as usual. "You fucking dumbass!" I shouted, dashing forward and tackling Spurgle against a concave slope in the stone wall. The rocks rained, except all but pebbles and dust were pushed out by the slope in the stone above. "Jesus, you about died, man. What was all that about?"

"I don't know!" shouted Spurgle, and I clapped my hand over his mouth for a second, finger to my lips to shush him, "Sorry. I just didn't realize it was dangerous."

"You didn't see the sign? We were talking about...right, you had earbuds in." I palmed my face in frustration.

Spurgle furrowed his Neanderthal brow. "It was a podcast about Yosemite. Did you know Abraham Lincoln was the one who—"

"Don't care." I turned around. "Wow, Mr. Wickerman, I thought that... Mr. Wickerman?" The red of his flannel jacket was mingled with the red blood pooling by his head. "Mister Wickerman is hurt!"

I glanced up, realizing that shouting wasn't the best idea right now, then dashed over. "What are you doing?" asked Spurgle.

"Checking his pulse." It beat so slowly, so faintly. "Weak. Shit." I checked his eyes. "Pupils are dilated. Wait, he's not breathing!"

Spurgle started gibbering in a way that belied language, doing a weird little dance like he had to piss or something. "What are you doing?" he asked again.

"CPR, stupid! Call nine-one-one!" I growled, then continued chest compressions and breathing into my boss's mouth, trying to jumpstart a man in his late middle years. He was healthy, though, so he should survive, I was sure of it.

"I don't have any bars!" whined Spurgle.

My heart jumped. "You were just listening to a podcast."

"I downloaded it to my phone!" He started pacing.

After another minute, Wickerman coughed. It felt like a miracle. With a groan, his eyes fluttered, and his head lolled to one side as he started to snore. "Shit. Holy shit. I did it. A man is going to live because of me." There was no time to linger on that, though, and I started rifling through the man's clothing.

"What are you—" Spurgle began.

"You don't have bars, which means I don't have bars, but Wickerman always carried...aha!" I withdrew a bulky brick from the pocket of Wickerman's flannel jacket. "Satellite phone!"

I made the call and, moments later, an ATV rolled up with two men and a trailer filled with medical equipment. After a doctor from the National Park Service examined him, it was decided that Wickerman's condition was too serious to just load him up and drive him to the nearest hospital. A helicopter was flown in to pick him up from the canyon floor. "Can I ride along? I mean, the man can't speak for himself. I was there. I know what happened."

"Sure," said the pilot. "What about this guy?"

"What do you say, Spurgle? Ride along or head to the cabin alone?" I asked, knowing the answer, except he didn't give it. Instead, Spurgle, avoiding eye contact, clumsily clambered into the chopper, a smell following him.

"Did...did you fart?" asked the pilot, grimacing.

"No," whined Spurgle.

"Well, I didn't fart, so... Wait, Spurgle?" The mewling manbaby merely nodded. The flight lasted forty-five minutes, but felt much, much longer.

∞

I sat and waited in the hospital room beside my boss, full of regret. Why didn't I help Wickerman? Why did I help Spurgle? The answer was obvious: Spurgle was about to be hit by rocks and I reflexively saved him. Wickerman wasn't in my line of sight, and I had no way of knowing the slope would shoot the stones at his head. For the first hour, it was just me and him, until Spurgle hunched into the room, smelling of bar soap.

You might be thinking that I'm being hard on the man, but trust me, I am not. "How is he?" asked Spurgle, pulling his wireless earbuds out of his ears. Again.

"It's a coma. He could wake up in a few minutes, a few days, maybe never. Sucks. I just wish...I wish I could've saved him from this, y'know?"

"Yeah, that would've been better," honked the moron, crunching a hospital vending machine candy bar.

"What? Dude, I couldn't save him because I was saving you." I rose to my feet, jabbing a finger in Spurgle's direction.

"No, you didn't. What are you talking about?" he asked, mouth full.

"What? Why do you think I tackled you!" A nurse ducked through the door, glaring at me. "Sorry! Sorry..."

"That's why you hit me? I thought you were just mad because I yelled." Spurgle chuckled, oddly detached from the situation.

"Are you...are you serious?" I asked. "Spurgle...there was a pile of rocks where you stood after I knocked you out of the way. The boss is in a coma from one rock. That pile would've killed you."

"No way..." he muttered, taking another bite, face blank and inscrutable like a sociopath's.

"Hm? What...what's going on?" came a voice from behind me. Wickerman was waking up!

"Oh, holy shit! Boss, you're awake!" I beamed, grabbing him by the face in disbelief as he squirmed. "Sorry, your head." I recoiled, having accidentally touched his bloody bandage. "Nurse!"

In came the same Nurse Ratchet-looking block of a woman, seemingly about to kick my ass. "You again!" Then, thankfully, she looked at Wickerman. "He's awake!" She dove in, examining his eyes, hitting the call button to get more of her people in the room. I breathed a sigh of belief. For a second, it really seemed like a lady who lifts sick people for a living was about to defenestrate me.

We were ushered out as a doctor arrived, and there was much chatter, but within five minutes, they scattered. "You can head back in. He's making a shocking recovery. Tough old bird. Don't linger; he's pretty tired, and with all the tests we have to run before discharging him, he's unlikely to want company."

I eagerly headed in, thankful that Wickerman's injuries weren't worse. "Bob! I mean, Mr. Wickerman. I'm so happy that you're okay. I thought you were gone for a minute there."

"Uh-huh," grunted the man I just saved. "Hey, is that Andy?"

"Yeah, boss, it's me. Andrew McMillan. You recognize me, right?" I glanced back, realizing he meant Spurgle.

"Hey boss." said Spurgle flatly, awkwardly. "Glad you're cool," he went on, removing earbuds again. I'd been talking to the man while we waited. This meant he hadn't heard a word I said.

"Yes, come here, son," said Wickerman. "The nurses told me what you did. Thank you. Thank you so much. Thank you for my life!"

I blinked, stunned. "Uh, sir. Actually, Spurgle here caused the rockslide that hurt you. You weren't breathing. I...I did CPR..."

The only reason I trailed off was the hard glare Wickerman was giving me. "They told me that *Andy* was the one who helped me, Mack. You're not Andy."

"But I am! When I gave my statement, I gave them my name. Andrew McMillan! Spurgle just panicked. For Chrissake, boss, he shat his pants while I gave you the breath of life!" I gesticulated, feeling foolish.

"Sad. Just sad, taking credit for another man's heroism. Next, you'll tell me that you created the Bluey Kazooey." He rolled his eyes at me, then turned to look at Spurgle.

Spurgle, with the chocolate smeared across his face like a toddler. Wickerman looked at him like a proud father regarding his son. "Y'know, maybe we should try relaunching that product. It probably would have sold some if we'd put more muscle into the advertising."

As the two men that I saved huddled together conspiratorially, I staggered out into the hall, in shock. A nurse caught me. "Sir, are you okay?" She checked my eyes. "You look ready to keel over."

"The man I saved hates me and thinks the man who caused his injury is a hero," I muttered.

"What? You mean that McMillan guy?" asked the nurse, putting a hand on her hip. "It was Andy that resuscitated him, right? That's what his chart says."

"Yes, that's me. Andrew McMillan. But he thinks it was Spurgle. I...he's an Andrew, too, but...he's also an idiot." I rubbed my face, which was hot, and no doubt very red.

"You sure you're okay?" she asked again, looking very concerned. I got the hell out of that hospital just shy of a running pace. I simply could not stand the injustice.

※

Taking the rest of the long weekend, I did all I could to disconnect, trusting that I'd be able to set things straight on Monday. Breaking out the navy pinstripe suit that got me the job in the first place, I returned to Malortech, refreshed. Sliding in early, the receptionist at the front desk stared at me. "Karen! Good morning." She waved back, numbly, grabbing her phone as I headed to the elevator. Odd.

Reaching my desk, I was greeted by Mr Wickerman. "Hey, boss, what's the good word?" I asked, trying to move into my cubicle, to unsling and hang my laptop case, in which I kept all the ideas I'd eventually flesh out and present to the company. I was ready to start the day strong.

But there was someone in my chair. "Hi!" said a bookish lady with round-lensed glasses. "I'm Janine." Janine smiled nervously, clearly still getting comfortable in her new position. I didn't recognize her.

"Sorry, Mack, but we've filled your old position," said Wickerman.

"What? But...my position wasn't empty. Boss, is this about the retreat? I... Spurgle!" My volume was a little out of control and drew more attention than I wanted. You could say that I was stressed.

"Yellow!" replied Spurgle, a single earbud in his left ear. I gritted my teeth.

"Tell Mr. Wickerman that I didn't cause his accident. I gave him CPR," I said, hands flailing.

"I mean...you did hit me," said Spurgle, stupidly.

Studying him intently, I searched what I knew of the man, comparing it to what I was seeing. "I tackled you out of the way of stones. Stones you brought down." My head swiveled between him and Wickerman. "Stones which injured our boss, Spurgle. Look at him! He has visible stitches on his head!"

"That's about enough out of you, Mack. You're lucky to still have this job." Wickerman glared.

My head was swinging around so much I started to get dizzy. Wickerman now clearly hated me, making no secret of his ire. Janine put on a headset as if she was taking a call, which was odd, since headsets aren't issued to employees. We're just not on the phone enough. Spurgle was still inscrutable! "You can't be serious. I...I'm a hero. I saved two lives!"

"I don't know, Mack. Seems to me that if you didn't hit me, if I didn't hit the rock wall, those rocks probably wouldn't have fallen." Finally, I saw it: a glint in Spurgle's eye. He was fighting back a smile. "No falling rocks, boss doesn't get hurt, y'know?"

With a harumph, Wickerman grabbed me by the shoulder, pulling me over one cubicle. "Enough already, Mack. Get away from Janine's cubicle. Frankly, it's a little untoward to be lingering near a lady's workspace."

I could do nothing but stutter, sounding like Spurgle panicking as I resuscitated Wickerman. I closed my eyes and focused on my breathing. When I opened my eyes, nothing had changed, though I'd been wishing it to be so.

"Why don't you get out of that jacket? Hell, take off your tie. As much running around as you'll be doing, you'll overheat otherwise. Leave them with Spurgle." As I stood, stunned, Wickerman stalked away. Turning back, Wickerman shouted, "Oh! In case it wasn't clear, your new title is Office Gopher. Now see if anybody needs anything. Chop-chop!" With a slam of the door, he disappeared into his office.

Slowly, I turned to look at Spurgle, shaking in silent laughter. Finally, when I found my voice again. "You...you did this on purpose. I saved your life and you ruined me. Why?"

Spurgle leaned back, putting his hands behind his head and putting his feet up on his desk. "Why, Mack, I have no idea what you mean. You heard the boss. You're lucky to even be here. I mean...you hit me, you injured Wickerman. Maybe just be glad nobody's pressing charges."

"You little shit—pants-shitting, after all I've put up with. You don't really think everybody's gonna believe this horseshit." I looked around at the office where I'd been a superstar for two years, at people who sang my praises, who came to me for input, and they all had their heads down. I was a pariah. I was toxic. They had to ignore me, or so they thought, because if they didn't, they'd pay the price.

"Poor Mack. No more Employee of the Month. Now...I'm the only Andrew in the office!" He started to laugh.

"Seriously?" I replied, grimacing. "You're not, though. My name didn't change. What's wrong with you?"

In reply, he merely laughed harder, then fell with a shout. "Ah! That was your fault! Get–get out of here! Get me a bagel! Sonderman's Bagels on fifth! Go!"

※

It was a two-block walk to Sonderman's, but I took half an hour, eating a bagel of my own and soaking up the WiFi. Sure, I was screwed. Nobody said my pay went down, though, that would have to come from HR. If I was still getting paid the same, I wasn't about to quit. Analyzing it, Spurgle must have done what he did out of self-preservation. Correcting the boss, taking responsibility...after the Bluey Kazooey, there's no way he wouldn't have been fired. Then getting rewarded with *my* rewards, he was just riding the wave. If he'd just told me that, showed some iota of moral fiber, I might have understood. But rubbing it in? I was pissed.

In that thrity minutes, I started a blog. VPN on, I created an email address, chose a blog service provider, one hosted on some island nation nobody'd ever heard of, and I went to work.

∞

"The Stupidity of Andrew Spurgle of 229 Wanton Way, Chicago, Illinois. Entry 1: Introduction.

"Hello, World,

"You may call me, merely, 'Truth Teller,' because I'm here to tell you the truth. The truth is that supervillains are real, really stupid, and, frankly, they smell bad. Meet one Andrew Spurgle: Supervillain."

I stared at the screen of my laptop, sipping coffee. This was libel, done quite purposefully. Did I really want to make myself vulnerable like this? Just to be safe, I ordered a second laptop, just like the first one. It took just a few minutes to find the same model. Conniving was fun. I started to understand Spurgle a little. Not enough to dissuade my taking revenge, but a little.

"Your Truth Teller has found a little nugget that helps form the origin story of this miserable malcontent, leech in human form, and explains why he's such a worthless piece of trash who should have been aborted. Not before he was born, mind you, but a very late-term abortion that takes place only after he has learned the meaning of pain.

"I know, you might be thinking, 'How cruel this Truth Teller is,' but trust me, I am not. You see, although his record has now been expunged, the young Spurgle was guilty of a great number of sins. I've obtained a comprehensive record of the boy's misdeeds, and let me tell you, today's is a doozy.

"That's right! To start, I've chosen the tale of Timmy, a little baby turtle that Mr. Spurgle, Andrew's father, brought home for him. Now you might think that pet stores are cruel places, little jails for baby animals, but this turtle was much better off at the pet store."

Pausing, I searched online, finding pictures posted of the Spurgle family. What luck! A picture of his cousin holding a tiny little box turtle. The family resemblance was enough to work, and just in case he started contacting family members, telling them to lock down online accounts, I set about downloading hundreds of pictures, videos and other stuff I could use in my quest for revenge. A quick Photoshop edit, and Andrew's cousin looked like a little demon, with the corners of his mouth pulled and his brow pinched, emoting on the concept of a demented clown.

"Receiving this turtle, Andrew's first instinct was to eat it, but Timmy bit down on Andrew's tongue. From there, it was hammertime. Lucky again, Timmy suffered no harm, weathering the beating from a baby's squeaky hammer with aplomb. But the four-year-old Andrew would not be denied. Timmy had a date with a firecracker and Andrew had a date with a psychiatrist. They locked him away for the detonation of little Timmy. It was Andrew's first stay in a padded cell, but it wouldn't be the last."

Picture attached, lies told, I hit "Post," and hustled back to work with bagels not just for Spurgle, but for the whole team, with enough cream cheese and jelly to go around. Yes, I sought to get my co-workers back on my side via bribery. So sue me.

"About time!" declared Spurgle. Then noting the large bag, "What is this?"

"Don't worry about it," I said, plopping a little box on his desk. "Raisin, right? There you go." Then, as he stood, watching, I delivered bagels to everyone else, even Janine, who now sat at my desk. Sheepishly, she took it. "I hope you like onion bagels," I said.

"Yes! I..." She trailed off, sniffing the hot, toasted goodness. "Sonderman's, huh?" As I moved down the line, I could hear the yummy noises as she consumed what I'd brought. All the while, Spurgle's eyes were upon me. He may have stolen my thunder, he may have buried me to the boss, but he couldn't cut my air supply. I would survive.

Months went by and my blog grew. Poking around on social media, I found Janine and her email address. Still masking my identity, I shot her a quick message, with a link, saying "I think you should look at this." To avoid being dismissed as SPAM, I made sure the title of the blog remained visible: "The Stupidity of Andrew Spurgle of 229 Wanton Way, Chicago, Illinois."

Within days, the whole team, then the whole office knew about the blog. Everyone except Spurgle and Wickerman, that is. This actually amplified the effect, because Spurgle wasn't smart enough to realize the office chatter was all about him and, without the boss's intervention, it could run rampant.

"*Entry 67: How Do You Make Something That Ugly Smell So Bad?*

"You would think that, at this point, I might run out of stories to tell about the felonious idiocy of the butcher of Wanton Way, but you'd be wrong. Yes, he murdered every childhood pet he ever had, yes, nobody can find any of his girlfriends from high school or college, but that doesn't mean he made them up. Maybe he killed them, too. If he, as a toddler, was willing to eat a live reptile, why wouldn't he, as an adult, eat a person? It's not a big jump.

"But let's stick to what's confirmed: his intelligence. As you no doubt know by now, the Spurgle is extremely stupid. Standardized tests failed to make contact with his brain, and so drastic measures had to be taken to understand what, exactly, was his malfunction.

"First, you must understand that he is a quarter bonobo, a kind of chimp. Don't get me wrong, I love animals, but not like grandma Spurgle loved chimpanzees. True, Andrew's father was short and hairy, but that doesn't mean he's part animal, does it? In answer to that, I'd just have to ask: does Spurgle really sound like a human name to you? No. No it does not.

"Bucky the Bonobo and Andrew's grandma had a short affair. She was a young zookeeper, he was a damned, dirty ape. He liked flinging feces, she was a coprophile. It was really a match made in heaven, or, at least, wherever good chimps go when they die.

"Now I need your help. I've heard a rumor that Bucky was, in fact, brother to Bubbles, a famous Chimp whom you may have seen hanging out in the 1980s with a well-known musician. If anyone could confirm this, I am offering them a $10,000 reward. Please send evidence to chimpfuckerspurgle@fake.com and, if acceptable, you will receive your reward in the form of 3.6 Chimpcoin."

It was about at this time that Spurgle became aware of the blog. I overheard the words spoken, though I don't know by who: "Is it true your grandpa was an ape?" In the moments that followed, there was an energetic conversation, terminating in a scream. I barely heard Spurgle's rage, as I'd decided it was a good time to take my lunch. A tuna sandwich eaten on a park bench had never tasted so good.

It had been almost a year and, by now, it became clear that Wickerman had recommended Spurgle for promotion. The slovenly toad had started dressing better, imitating my own fashion decisions, going to the same tailor (not paranoia—Laslo told me Spurgle had been there). Long story short: I began to have a crisis of conscience. My parents might try to guide me to be a better person, so I called my grandmother, to confess and get her opinion.

Grandma Mary was born in Glasgow, and while she'd been a beauty in her youth, she was a stout beauty, and loved fighting. Fighting men. She was also the most vindictive woman to ever set foot in Chicago. If they're to be believed, Grandma was about to beat my grandpa senseless when he presented her with a bouquet of flowers and a ring. He'd admired her from afar as she sent men to the hospital. She never beat up another woman that I was aware of; they all ran the second she cocked back her fist.

"Ah, baby, I'm glad you came to me for this. Sounds like you're doin' a great job." God, I love my grandma.

"Are you sure, Granny Mary? I mean, I know how you'd handle it…" I said, fishing for reassurance.

"What you have on your hands there, boy, is what in the old country, we called a 'falach'd.' It's a Gaelic word that translates to somethin' like 'blood feud.' To end the falach'd, you have to avenge the wrong done to ya. Otherwise, you'll be haunted for all time!"

I grinned. "Blood feud? Okay. And I should stay, uh, sneaky?"

Her tone ticked up a note. "Oh, sure, you could be direct, feed the man his teeth, but I'm glad you walked away. You're buildin' a career! Your grandpa, he had the career, designin' brownstones and the like. Me, I kept your daddy and his heathen siblings in line. Every one of them turned out great, and so did you."

The guilt I felt faded. "Thanks, Granny Mary, you're the best."

"You bet, kiddo. Now, remember though, if you can get him to swing first, all bets are off. Then you can whip him like an untrained donkey! And get out to the 'burbs every now and then. We miss ya."

We said our goodbyes and I sat there for a moment, scheming. The Bluey Kazooey relaunch was this Saturday, four pm, and Spurgle would be giving a presentation to the entire company. By now, virtually everyone in the building was following the Stupidity blog. I could tell by the timing of the audible notifications they received on their phones. I had to come up with a post, something to finish the job, and it had to be right as he began his presentation. At twenty-five after the hour, he should have started but couldn't possibly be finished talking—that's when I'd strike.

∞

The post written, I scheduled it for the precise moment when I thought it would have the greatest effect. That night, before drifting off, I hit "Post," laughing all the way to Dreamland.

"*Entry 192.*

"It's all been building up to this, folks. The facts of the case painted a picture, and the picture is this blog entry that you're reading now. The truth can finally be told: Andrew Spurgle is the Chicago Strangler.

"I know, it sounds like a stretch, but remember that the Strangler was thought to be more than one man. While Spurgle is a weak, feckless little man with the spine of a jellyfish, the Strangler's victims were all women. True, most of those women would definitely have killed Spurgle in self-defense easily, but you forget that Andrew Spurgle's father is half-ape!

"'Where's the proof,' you ask? Rest assured, I have it in spades, and I will be presenting it in the near future. There are genomic test results showing that Spurgle is a lower lifeform, not altogether human! Security footage from 2015 shows a teenage Spurgle strangling a victim alongside his father. At this point, the younger Spurgle has not started shaving his ape-fur off, but it is him! The truth must come out.

"Just last week, his locker at the Northside College Preparatory High School was found to contain the bloody clothes of one victim. Want more truth? We have the locker number. It's 272! That's second floor, locker Seventy-Two. Undeniable!

"The final proof: just look at this video of a teenage Andrew Spurgle dancing at his Junior Prom dance. Tell me that's not the dance of a simian, subhuman murderer. You cannot!"

There. It was lowbrow, it was underhanded, terrible, really, but it would do.

I'd started to realize since Spurgle fooled Wickerman with his blatant lie that people were not nearly so smart as I'd always imagined. Primacy bias, the tendency to believe the first thing you're told, kept Wickerman from listening to me. He couldn't understand I was the Andy who saved him because he thought of me as "Mack," my nickname proving my own undoing.

Then, worst of all, confirmation bias caused him to dismiss anything he'd hear against Spurgle or in favor of me. Add to that the fact that my method of fighting back, this blog, had convinced most of the staff at Malortech. Even a month before this post would have seemed like too much, but my lies had primed everyone to believe anything the blog said. At this point, if I kept being so successful at deceiving people, I decided I should run for office. It was the natural next step. The psychotic, raving lunatics that left comments on my blog, showed me that people would believe anything. Someone's going to take advantage, so why shouldn't it be me?

∞

Saturday was normally a day off, but still, I didn't mind heading into Malortech that evening. Starting the event, Wickerman was there to set up Spurgle for success. "Welcome! And thank you to everyone for coming in on a Saturday. A little over a year ago, a brilliant mind brought a concept that few people believed in and, frankly, it wasn't given a chance. It did poorly in the test markets and the plug was pulled, but now, I really think it's time. But first, let me recap the first three decades here at Malortech."

It was the first of several long-winded speeches about stupid plastic crap. The Bluey Kazooey wasn't going to be our only new product for the calendar year, but you wouldn't know it the way Wickerman went on. Finally, the VP in charge of Marketing came on, talking Spurgle up, and I realized something was off.

This normally verbose man, someone who projected power, was antsy. He stuttered, projected fear, and was sweating in a way I could see from my seat in the fifth row. He was a reader. There could be no doubt: I'd terrorized this man into thinking that Spurgle, the man who stole my life, really was a monster.

Checking my watch, it was 4:24pm, and my eyes grew as the Vice President on stage finally found his strong voice, proclaiming, "And now, your man of the hour... Andrew Spurgle!"

I couldn't restrain the beaming grin plastered across my face. The screen of my watch showed the seconds, and I counted them down as Spurgle took the stage. "Thank you, Gene! Hey, everybody! It's so great to talk up here to you all about stuff. It's about time my idea got the attention that I should have gotten from day one around here. Keep in mind that, when I got here, it was cold. Every day has been warmer. Coincidence?"

Tuning him out (who couldn't? He sounded both stupid and crazy), I held my breath as the minute turned over. 7:25. Panic. No notification. He was rambling again. I couldn't believe it. There's no way he could keep up this nonsense; he wasn't a speaker. Already, I could see him backing towards the VP, who waited to applaud the product's re-introduction, and who backed away from him in fear. Then it happened.

First it was a single ding, a few seats behind me. Spurgle, like the sociopath he was, stopped talking. "You people are supposed to have your phones turned *down*! You're ruining my big moment!"

A second ding. A third! Many more people were checking their phones than there were dings; they must be set to vibrate! My own phone went off. Entry 192. There it was, a link on my watch screen.

People were reading. The VP was reading. "Oh my God!" he shouted, jumping off the stage, then backing away, afraid to take his eyes off the "Strangler."

"Where are you going?" He looked all over, seeing all the screens illuminating the faces of every man and woman in the auditorium. "It's...it's that blog, isn't it? What is it? What does it..." He got his own phone out. "If I ever figure out..." He blanched.

It was a short entry, so in seconds, everyone had read and was digesting. They were horrified, and far, far too many believed it to be literally true. I couldn't contain myself any longer. "Can you believe it?" I cackled as I shook the guy in front of me by the shoulders. He looked back, horrified, which I found hysterical.

"You!" shouted Spurgle, jumping down and nearly falling on his face. "It's been you all along, hasn't it?" The people in front of me, three whole rows, scattered, and quickly, I was alone in my own row. "Andrew fucking McMillan!"

I was alone, but not afraid. "What? Little old me? I'm not even here, right? You're 'the only Andrew in the office,' right?"

It was never true. Andrew was a stupidly common name. Hell, there were five on our floor. Still, he knew this was a confession, and one that only he would understand. "You... I'll kill you!"

He fell over the first row of seating, rolled awkwardly over the second, then reached over the third to grab my waiting throat. I welcomed the assault, pulling away only after he had a grip, helping him to get over me. I swam regularly for cardio exercise, and my lungs were full; I had oxygen to spare. I gagged out a few words to really sell it.

"Help!" I gasped. "The Chicago Strangler is strangling me!" Finding their balls, our security force mobbed Spurgle, and he was dragged off me, screaming. By now, Wickerman was back on the stage, watching the show in shock.

As Spurgle was pulled away, I clutched my own throat, making sure that it looked like the weakling Spurgle had actually left a mark. As Wickerman approached, I was overjoyed to see that he'd nicked me with those nasty, chewed nails of his. "What the fuck was that, Mack?" he demanded.

"It's like I told you last year, sir!" I coughed. "He's crazy. He attacked you on the retreat and then pinned it on me!"

"Oh...oh no," he muttered. "I wanted to diversify, to get away from sunglasses and kazoos. Why did I think a combination of the two was a good idea?"

"It's not your fault, sir. You were under his spell. He really is a bad man. There's a whole blog about it. Here, I'll send you a link." Let me tell you, they hadn't even gotten Spurgle to the jail before he was unemployed.

∞

I didn't go into politics after all. Now that Wickerman understood who saved him and who hurt him (even if the "attack" was exaggerated), now that I was the victim of an attack on company property, I was all set. Quickly, I led my own team, and as of right now, I'm being considered for a vacant VP chair.

Of course I pressed charges. He may have been agitated, he may have been entrapped, but Spurgle really was a bad man. He'd already hurt one man just by virtue of his stupidity, he attacked me over posts on the Internet, and there was this weird rumor online about him being a serial killer. The assault would mean a six-month sentence but the investigation that ultimately exonerated him of all the Chicago Strangler murders? That would take years. We live in a stupid society, people, and it may seem crazy, but these things do happen.

Believe me, I read it on the Internet.

You Stand Accused

Sarah Arnette

You Stand Accused

"Andrew Spurgle, you stand accused of antiquities theft. You have been found in possession of the rare and culturally significant Kong, from the region of Golden, Colorado," the woman in the front of the room booms.

She is a good boomer. Moms are like that: they can make the smallest infraction a major ordeal. My mom is the master at it. She might be little for a human, only twice my height and weight, but she doesn't know it. I'd describe what she looks like, but most humans look the same to me. You all smell different, though, so I'll describe that. Mom smells like flowers and love, except for right now. Right now, she smells like flowers and anger.

The room is the living room. For this purpose, it is also known as the Courtroom. The black couches have been pushed back, exposing an open area of the living room floor and its fancy carpet. It is fancy, not because it is colorful, which it is, but rather because NOTHING sticks to it. You spill anything, and it comes right up. That is a fancy carpet. I digress—back to the Courtroom.

Dad is standing bailiff. He is standing at the back of the room, just waiting for me to bolt. He's taller than Mom, which isn't that hard for a human. He smells like soap and resignation. He doesn't want to be here doing this. He would rather be watching television. I'd rather he be watching television.

I have a lawyer, Tommy Squishes. He's a Boston Terrier/something mix. He's got the round head of a Boston, and the colors of one, but he's way too tall and has wire-like fur. His round head gives him more room for a brain, which is why he is my lawyer. I'm gonna need a really good one to get out of this predicament. Oh, and he is also my brother, so he has something of a stake in this. I swear it's not a conflict of interest for my brother to defend me. That's what brothers are supposed to do.

The accuser is the problem. That honor goes to my sister, Mabel Swabbles. Yeah, we all have different last names. Humans, go figure. We all have the same parents, but completely different last names. Mabel is the baby of the family and is treated accordingly. Anything she wants, she gets. Right now, what she wants is revenge because I stole the Kong. It is an antique: it belongs in a museum, not in her dirty little paws.

You see, Mabel is a literal baby. She is six months old and does not know how to chew things nicely. She is teething, and everything she touches is destroyed. If she doesn't learn now how to chew nicely, then she'll be a holy terror when she is a year old. Pitbulls have strong teeth. Trust me, I know.

Back to the trial. I really should be paying attention. Mom is glaring at me. Dad lets out a sigh. He's caught me just looking around, blankly. "Andy, are you gonna pay attention at all? You're not helping your case," Tommy says. He's trying to whisper it to me, but he does not realize how loud he is. Everyone's heard him.

"I'm listening, I'm listening. I swear," I reassure him. I was not listening. I never listened. That is why we have so many of these trials.

"Sure, what did Mom just say?"

"Um...that I am accused?" I guessed. I know at some time she must have said this. Judging from the look that Tommy is giving me, that's not what she said. I really should learn to pay attention.

"Mom has moved to begin the trial. She asked how you plead, but you didn't answer her. She's ready to hold you in contempt. I wouldn't blame her if she gave you The Business for not paying attention." Tommy sounded shaken by the idea of The Business.

The Business is one of the many punishments Mom gives out that Dad does not. The Business is when she pulls you aside and either yells at you, which is bad, or talks to you, which is worse. When she yells, she is frustrated. When she just talks, she is disappointed.

"What happens next?" I ask Tommy. I should know. There've been a million of these courts, but I never pay attention.

"Mom is going to call for the Prosecutor to present her evidence and witnesses. You are not to say a word. You got it?" Damn, Tommy is being so bossy today. You would think he would have some type of trust in me. I mean, it's not like he hasn't been my lawyer from the start, oh so many years ago. Oh, wait, that might be why he has no faith in me.

"The Prosecutor...that's Mabel, right?"

"No, it's worse. Amilia Bajilia has gotten involved and has taken the case on, gratis."

"Amilia Bajilia? For real?" How did I not notice her? Amilia is ancient. She never takes a case anymore. Normally you find her in the stands, watching the court from the comfort of the couches. If she's involved, I am going to be in so much trouble. Her chihuahua brain might be small, but it is mighty. Her bug eyes see everything. She is fierce and aggressive with her arguments. You would never know she was all of four pounds with how she handles herself in a debate.

The Prosecutor

Amilia steps forward to the center of The Court, standing before Judge Mom. Her steps are slow and cautious. She trembles a little bit as she stands there. She is wearing her customary pink sweater and headband. On some dogs, this might make them appear weak or silly. On Amilia, all it does is make her appear ancient and wise. It reminds me a lot of those tracksuits that the senior citizens wear at the hospital we visit. Those people can be tough, too.

"Your honor and other members of this court, I am Amilia Bajilia. I have come out of retirement to represent the case of my dear sister, Mabel Swabbles. In this case about a pup who could not control his own greed, a young and innocent baby has been grievously injured.

"While she might not bleed, she may not limp, her soul cries in pain, and her confidence is shattered. She was entrusted with the care and use of the most valued and sought-after artifact of the old era: the Kong. It was ruthlessly stolen from her by a villain who claims to be trying to protect it for the future. In truth, Andrew Spurgle, known felon and violator of the peace, simply took it for his use and benefit." Not once does Amilia's voice tremble, even as her entire body shook with age, and the fact that she's a chihuahua.

Tommy and I sit there, at a complete loss. We did not see this coming. She's made me sound like I'm out to cause harm or something. She even makes it sound like there's some type of profit in protecting the Kong. I put it in the museum, but I do not get any use from it. Granted, I might have chewed it a little bit, but that's what happens when you don't have hands to carry things with. Yes, the museum is next to my bed, but it is still in the common part of the house. It's not like I stop anyone from looking at the items in the museum.

There are a lot of things in my...I mean, the museum. I have the very first cow hoof that Mom ever gave me, slightly chewed. I have the tail end of a couple of rope toys, splinters of bones, and even a nylon bone in there. I keep them so the rest of the dogs in the family can see what types of toys we have been playing with and how they have been replaced. You know, cultural things. Important things. More important than little Miss Mabel and her getting her own way all the time.

"In this trial, I will prove that Andrew Spurgle is guilty of the crimes of antiquity theft, burglary, and simple assault. I will use not only eyewitnesses, but also tangible proof of his crimes. While he may think he's in the right or that he is preserving the past for the future, it's the present that he should be most concerned with, for it is in the present that he shall pay for his sins against his sister." Holy crap, Amilia has increased the number of charges I have been accused of by threefold.

"Hey now! That's not fair," I shout to her. "You can't add more charges to me! I already have one too many." Her cold look of disdain should have warned me, but hey, if I'm going to go down, I'm going to go down hard.

"Andy! Shut up," Tommy stage-whispers to me. He does not want to go down with me.

Thinking fast, I call to Judge Mom, "I object!" This works on the television, so it should work now. Despite the hundreds of trials I have been in here, I have never actually needed to defend myself. I let Tommy do it, but this is against Amilia.

"Overruled," Judge Mom calmly, almost sounding bored, calls back. Is she even taking this seriously?

"I object to the overrule!" I am not letting this go.

"Andy! Shut Up!" Tommy doesn't even pretend to whisper this time. It is getting loud in the court.

"Andrew Spurgle, you will maintain your peace, or you will have to leave this court and the trial will continue without you." That's Bailiff Dad. He would put me outside to cool my heels while the trial continues. If he does that, then I'd have to leave my whole case up to Tommy. He's smart, but Amilia is smarter. I'd lose for sure. I have to make sure I stick around and help Tommy defend me.

As I am thinking about this, I replay what Amilia said. She said she had witnesses to me rescuing the Kong from certain destruction. But who could these witnesses be? I made sure there was no one else around, that it was just Mabel and myself. Antiquities procurement can be tricky, so making sure it goes smoothly is a major part of my planning session. After all, uncivilized beings like baby sisters can damage the items if they are not handled carefully, and the more savages involved, the higher the chance of a problem. Amilia also mentioned proof. Surely, she was not going to dangle the Kong as proof. We all know it goes to the library. What proof could she be talking about?

The Witnesses

Amilia is pulling out all the stops in this case. It's not even that big of a deal. It's a Kong. Yes, it is The Kong, from Golden, Colorado. Yes, it's storied in the lore that it was carried here from the lands of sun and mountains by a white Golden Retriever. Yes, there is a legend that this Golden Retriever will come back someday to retrieve his Kong and grant everyone replenishing treats, but no one actually believes in that stuff.

"Your Honor, may I please present my very first witness, Max," Amilia announces to the room in general. As she says his name, Max steps in from the kitchen. This means he comes through the back of The Courtroom and past Bailiff Dad, who must not have known that Max is here, because he jumps when he hears Max's claws tapping on the floor. Judge Mom frowns, but she allows Max to come into The Courtroom.

Max is the neighbor's dog. He's an old mastiff type of dog. His breed has a fancy French name, but no one can ever pronounce it right. He's a big dog, fitting for a name like Max. He is built to the Max, and he drools to the Max. He is also my cohort in squirrel chasing. We are going to have words, depending upon his testimony today.

"Now, Max, you claim that you saw Andrew take the Kong from Mabel?" Amilia starts right in with her questioning.

"Yes, I saw Andrew take the Kong." Max's voice is deep and loud. It's a shocking contrast to Amilia's high-pitched voice.

"Can you describe what happened?"

"I object!" I shout before Max could begin his testimony. Why isn't Tommy doing this?

"Overruled," Judge Mom says. She sounds like she expected me to object.

"But there's no way that Max saw anything! I know, be—"

"Andy! Shut up," Tommy cuts me off. I open my mouth again, but he just snaps at me. "No, shut up."

"Please continue, Max," Judge Mom invites.

"Anyway, I saw Andrew take the Kong from Mabel, who was sitting in the sun on the Deck, chewing on the toy. Then Andrew looked around as though he was making sure no one was around, nipped Mabel's ear to distract her, and then took the toy while she was looking around and behind her," Max testifies.

"And where were you when this occurred?" Amilia asks.

"I was on my Deck, also enjoying the sun."

"Andrew did not see you when he looked around?"

"I don't think he looked over at our deck. I think he was just looking for you and Tommy."

"You think, but you don't know this?" Amilia wants to clarify this for the Court. She doesn't want to leave any loopholes open that I could jump through, because she knows I'm good at jumping. I'm a German Shepherd, and we're an athletic breed.

"There is no way to know for sure what goes on in Andrew's head. He is always full of great ideas and weird applications."

"HEY! I represent that!" I interrupt.

"I think you mean you resent that, but your statement is correct either way," Amilia snips. She might have me there. I'm pretty sure I have been insulted, though. Judge Mom should put a stop to that.

"Mom! Amilia is being mean to me!" I call to her. Crap, I forget her title for this Court. I should have said, *Judge Mom*. Hopefully, she lets it slide. I also should have said that I object. Court procedures are so complicated.

"Sustained. Amilia, keep it professional." Finally, Mom rules something in my favor.

"So you suspect that Andrew was not looking for you." Amilia corrects her question, getting back on track after the interruption.

"No, I do not suspect that Andrew was looking for me," Max answers.

"What did Mabel do when she noticed that Andrew took the Kong from her?"

"Mabel cried. She was enjoying chewing on the Kong. I don't blame her. Kongs are great toys to chew on, especially when you are teething like she is. She tried to get it back from Andrew, but he is taller than she is and held it over her head where she couldn't reach it. Then he ran away with it, leaving her on the Deck without anything to play with."

"Do you feel that Mabel's reaction was justified?"

"Yeah, if it were me, I would be upset, too, if Andrew took one of my toys. Especially if he then teased me by holding it over my head before running away with it."

"Hey! I did not—" I begin, but Tommy interrupts me again.

"Shut up, Andy!"

"Andrew, you will have your chance to talk and defend yourself. For now, please, hold your peace," Judge Mom says. "Max, Amilia, please continue." I lay down while I listened to them continue to explain the events on the Deck, poorly. It's going to be a long trial and I'm going to have to work to keep my strength up for it. Maybe there will be a cookie break. Then I would have a chance to have a word with Max about what he thinks he saw.

"I think I'm done with Max. I would like to call my second witness, Brutus." Amilia surprises the Court with that statement. There's another dog in the house? Brutus soon comes tip-tapping his way into the Courtroom. He's Max's brother, a Wheaten Terrier. Where Max fills in his name and then some, Brutus is tiny. It's hard to believe that they were brothers, but then again, I have a chihuahua, a Boston Terrier, and a pit bull as siblings, so what can I say?

"Are there more dogs in the kitchen?" Judge Mom calls over to Bailiff Dad. She seems rather confused as to how the neighbor's dogs got into the house. I think Amilia convinced Mabel to open the door. Mabel might be the baby, but she is tall enough to reach doorknobs, and Amilia is smart enough to have figured out how to open the door. That's a trick I will definitely need to learn, if that's the case.

Bailiff Dad turns the corner from the living room—I mean Courtroom—and looks into the kitchen. "It appears we have all of the neighbor's dogs here. Circe and No One are also here." Bailiff Dad no longer sounds surprised to find more dogs in the house.

"Their mom is gonna have a fit when she discovers them gone. At least she'll be glad we have them rather than them wandering the streets. I'll have to give her a call once this is done to let her know. She should be at work, which might be why she hasn't called us yet. She most likely doesn't even know they're not home." Judge Mom rubs her hands over her face. That is a clear sign that Mom is getting tired and frustrated. That's not good for my chances of getting out of this.

"Brutus, did you see Andrew take the Kong from Mabel?" Amilia starts as soon as Brutus sits down in front of Judge Mom.

"No, I did not." His answer is crisp and clear. His voice is just a shade deeper than Amilia's and like crystal. He does affect a little bit of an accent, but no one knows where that accent was supposed to be from. He once said it was from England, but I am pretty sure he's never been out of the city. Unlike me, I've been everywhere in my hunt for valuable antiques.

"Did you see Andrew with the Kong at any point of the day?"

"Yes, I saw him carrying the Kong from the Deck into the house just a few minutes ago, maybe half an hour ago, now."

"I obj—" I start to say, but again, Tommy interrupts me.

"Shut up, Andy. Anything you say might incriminate yourself," Tommy says. His tone is sharp with me. I might have irritated him with all of my interruptions. I do not argue with him, just put my head down on my paws.

"Did you hear or see anything that makes you think that he might have taken it away from Mabel?"

"Yes. I saw Mabel carry the Kong out onto the deck ten minutes before I saw Andrew with it. I also heard her crying and fighting with him right before I saw Andrew carry it inside."

"Thank you, Brutus. Please stay in case we need you for further testimony." Amilia dismisses him. "As further evidence, I would like to present the Kong itself." At that, Amilia goes behind the couch and pulls out the Kong in question. It's the same one from my museum! She stole it from me. I immediately jump up to get it, but Tommy and Brutus jump between us. Max eventually manages to stand up, too. Two-on-one I might have handled, but three-on-one is too much. I sit back down. Amilia could have it, for now. I would get it back.

"Ladies and gentlemen of the Court, please notice the chew pattern on the Kong. As you can see, there are small bite marks where Mabel was enjoying the toy. Overlapping these are the much heavier marks caused by a much stronger dog with bigger teeth, much like the ones Andrew has. There are also scratch marks where you could clearly see that Mabel attempted to get the Kong back from Andrew.

"This was an aggressive act of theft, not a pleasant trade of toys. Andrew took advantage of her size and stole what rightfully belonged to her by the laws of possession. I rest my case." Amilia drives that last statement like a nail in my coffin. It's looking pretty bad.

I Can Explain

"All right, Andrew. Do you care to explain? It is not looking good for you right now," Judge Mom says. She's right: the evidence does point to my guilt, but I can explain. I take a deep breath, and I am just about to begin when Tommy interrupts again.

"Andy, shut up. Don't say anything. I think this is called entrapment when they get you to say or do something to incriminate yourself." Tommy almost sounds like he knows what he is doing. Maybe I should listen to him? He is my counsel, and Mom says it is good to listen to wise counsel. Then I remember that Tommy likes to pee on the spiny thing, getting pee everywhere, even on him. He also likes to eat bunny poop. He might not be the wise counsel that Mom is referring to.

"No, no, I got this," I tell him. After all, I have managed to talk myself out of trouble maybe six times so far. Yeah, I'm in trouble a lot more often, but I do have a record of success to maintain. This is going to be success number seven. I can just feel it.

Turning to look at the Court, I plaster a giant smile on my face. It is my best smile, with my front teeth showing and my eyes almost shut. This smile alone gets me out of so much trouble. For some reason, it does not appear to be having the desired effect on the Court, so I turn to Judge Mom, and begin my tale.

"I can explain everything," I start. "It all started when I was just a puppy..." I swear the heavenly harps begin to play. They don't do that for the guilty, do they? I think not. "Back when I was a cold, homeless little puppy..." Is that Sarah McLachlan singing in the background? "I came across a display window. In that display window, they were playing a movie: Indiana Jones. Through his adventures spent over the next hour and a half, I learned that I had a passion for preserving the past through archaeology. Attending college, where I got to meet the famous professor, I soon learned all that I needed to know to assess, and then preserve relics of the past. Having proven my dedication to the field, I was allowed to follow Indiana Jones on many adventures, meeting his friend Chewbacca, and exploring galaxies.

"In short order, our museum was filled with culturally important, valuable finds. We managed to dupe the Nazis, secure the Rebel bases from the Empire, and with the accusation of The Kong, we paved the way for the Golden Retriever to return from the lands of Colorado. It is my fevered hope that this will sway you in your judgments.

"It was as I watched the uncultured swine chew on the priceless relic of a bygone era that I knew I had to act. Channeling my inner adventurer, I devised a daring plan. I snuck up behind the unsuspecting savage tribal member. I checked, and then double-checked for traps, but there were none to be seen. Sneaking along the deck, I was careful not to step on any of the cracks, as they might be slots for the spears designed to impale trespassers.

"Finally, I had to reach deep into my memories of being a street urchin and devise a way to trick my unsuspecting mark to get the Kong from her tiny grubby paws. Using sleight of hand, I tickled her ear, causing her to turn around in surprise, leaving the Kong unattended. With the speed of the wind and the grace of a rolling stream, I snatched up the Relic and made my escape.

"It was a harrowing escape, at that. The whole tribe of savages chased me down the bank, biting and scratching at me. I was certain that if I didn't get away, they would eat me. Luckily, I had my escape vehicle not too far away, and was able to jump in and close the door before they caught me. The Relic was a little banged up, they had put some scratches on it, but I figured I could buff those out once we got to the museum. It was only once it was safely behind glass that I could relax."

"Andy, shut up," Tommy says before I begin describing the other items in my museum. He looks almost sick. It's definitely because he knows he could never make such an amazing speech. I look around the room, expecting to see downcast eyes of defeat, but that is the opposite of what I'm greeted with. Why is Amilia smiling? Why does Judge Mom have her head in her hands? Did I mess up? No, never.

"Andy, you just confessed to the crime that they accused you of. You confessed to taking the Kong," Tommy explains. Oh. I fluff up.

"Andrew Spurgle, you do know that what you described was a combination of the plot to *Indiana Jones and the Temple of Doom* and *Star Wars*, right? Indiana Jones isn't real, and neither is Han Solo. Chewbacca does not exist, and you most certainly did not attend college or travel the galaxy," Amilia says accusingly.

"Han Solo exists!" There is the potential that I might have confused my life with a story, but I know Han Solo exists. He lives with his sister Leia down the block. They're French Bulldogs.

With a giant sigh, Amilia clarifies her statement. "Han Solo and Indiana Jones in the character formats you portrayed do not exist. Yes, there is a dog named Han Solo. I can assure you, he has not traveled the galaxy, even if I cannot be sure he does not have a friend named Chewbacca. They have a lot of friends with weird names, like Kilo and Rey.

"Judge Mom, I rest my case." Amilia ends with another giant sigh. She lies down on the floor, and proceeds to take a nap. I just know I'm in trouble.

The Verdict

Judge Mom said she would deliberate, confer with Bailiff Dad, and examine all of the evidence before she makes a final verdict. While this happens, Amilia leads Mabel over to the side to discuss their options, depending upon what Judge Mom decides. Max, Brutus, Circe, and No One help themselves to the treat bin, and I'm left with Tommy.

Boston Terrier mixes are not well-known for being shaky. Tommy might be one of the most steadfast dogs I've ever met. He's not afraid of anything and never has any worries. There is only one thing that ever scares him, and that is when Mom gives him The Business. Tommy looks rather shaken and maybe a little scared now.

"What's the plan?" I ask. After all, he is my counsel. I'm sure he has something of a plan.

"Plan? The plan was going to be for me to throw us upon the mercy of the court with the evidence and witness testimony so stacked against us. But then you decided to go off and give everyone a crazy piece of fan-fiction life story. You buried us. There is no way you're not going to be found guilty. There's even a likely chance you'll be made an example of, given the max sentence. I might even share that sentence because I am over here representing you. All because you couldn't keep your mouth shut." Tommy hunches down, looking mournfully over at Judge Mom. You would almost believe that he's looking at the possibility of having to go to Dog Prison. We're not, right?

"Hey, um...what is the max sentence for something like this?" Being given The Business, I can handle it. Yeah, I don't like it when Mom yells at me, but it's some type of attention, so it's okay. Sometimes I get put on Time-Out, and that's when I have to sit apart from everyone. That's the worst. Mom never hits me, unless I'm doing something dangerous and she wants me to never do it again, like when I got on the stove. Like, I was literally standing on the stove, doing her dishes, and she smacked my butt. I've never done that one again. The idea of Dog Prison has never even crossed my mind until now.

I've been to Dog Prison. All of us have. It is a scary place with a lot of dogs and cats. We are all locked in these kennels without any parents to hold us and love us. We don't even have any friends to share the kennel with. We are all alone. Yeah, there is a roof over our heads and food in our bellies, but that is just what a puppy needs to survive. There is so much more that a pup needs to live. It's better than the streets, though, which is where I did spend the first few months of my life. Tommy and I both spent time on the streets, but Mabel and Amilia were dumped by their families, sent to Dog Prison, so I know it can happen.

"You're a reoccurring felon, so you might be sent to Dog Prison. It's doubtful, though," Tommy answers after a moment's thought. "Mom, or Judge Mom, is not a fan of sending pups to Dog Prison. She says it's far more effective to do rehab and training in the home than simply sending a dog away. Most likely you will get Time Out. How long your Time Out is will depend upon how much Amilia argues for and how hurt Mabel is. You might be looking at upwards of twenty minutes."

"Twenty minutes! A dog can expire left in Time Out for twenty minutes!" That is ludicrous. I did not actually hurt Mabel. There is not a mark on her. Surely the punishment will not be so extreme. "What about the

Relic? What will they do with the Kong?" I have completely forgotten about that. With any luck, it will be returned to the museum. It is a piece of history, and it needs to be protected. Without it, the Golden Retriever might never return, bringing with him cookies and snacks.

"Oh, that? It will most likely be returned to Mabel. She was the one playing with it." Tommy is far less concerned about the Kong than I am.

"Will you make an argument that it should go to my...I mean, the museum?" I am frantic. I'm so upset that the Kong might be lost that my lips get stuck on my teeth while I'm talking. I have to bark a few times to get them free. Judge Mom and Bailiff Dad look over at me when I do this, and they don't look pleased. Amilia and Mabel do, though.

"Argue for you keeping the Kong? No. I don't think I will. We're already in trouble. I think we should just take the loss."

"But if we just take the loss, then everything we went through has been in vain! What was even the point of me rescuing the Kong if Mabel is just given it at the end of all of this? That would be so unfair, being punished and I can't even keep what I was punished for taking. Who ever heard of such a thing?"

"Andy, you do realize what you did was a crime, right? You stole from a *baby*. You're going to do the time, and she's going to get reparations. Those reparations will include either the item or something of the item's value in consolation."

"But it's priceless!"

"As you say, brother. As you say," Tommy sighs. There is no reasoning with me when I get this way.

Reparations

The ending of the trial is just as Tommy predicted. "Andrew Spurgle, this Court has found you guilty of Antiquities Theft. There is no evidence to indicate Assault on your sister, Mabel, so in that, you are found not guilty. As for burglary, you live here, so you did not unlawfully enter the premises. In that charge, you have been found innocent. Amilia, it is recommended that if you are going to continue to practice law, you brush up on those laws that you suggest," Judge Mom pronounces.

I haven't been paying that much attention to what has been going on in the Court after talking to Tommy. I haven't even realized that the Court has reconvened. I'm apparently the only one who hadn't noticed. The fact that my lips are once again stuck on my teeth doesn't help me look like I know what's going on. Unfortunately, I don't have time to unstick my lips, so I'm going to have to listen to my sentencing looking like a goofball.

"Do you have anything to say for yourself?" Oh! Judge Mom is going to give me a chance to plead for the fate of Kong! I might be able to get it into the museum, after all. I have to think fast.

"Your Honor, might I plead on the behalf of my client, Andrew Spurgle? He begs for leniency in this case. He is a very good boy who sometimes makes bad decisions and allows his imagination to get away from him. We humbly ask that his punishment be conditionally suspended, with the stipulation that he does not bother Mabel again today or go after the Kong," Tommy quickly says. He's good. I know all those words, but I don't know them all together. But then it dawns on me what he said.

As Judge Mom considers his request, this is my very last chance to see the Kong to safety. "Your Honor, Mother! Please, that Relic belongs in a museum. Think of the children, of the future. Someday, the Golden Retriever shall return, and we must have the Kong ready for him or else we will not receive the bounty of his treats. Please, demand that Mabel relinquishes it to the museum," I plead.

Tommy takes a good look at me as soon as I'm done making my statement to the court. He doesn't look pleased at all. Maybe I should have reminded him to have the Court give me the Kong. After all, if I'm gonna get in trouble, it might as well be worth it. Right before Judge Mom hands down the sentence, he lunges at me.

Holy Biscuits, I don't see that coming. Tommy has never been an angry dog. I'm not even sure what I did to push him over the edge. Granted, he doesn't hurt me. He just pushes me and starts barking really loud. I'm not stupid: I back right up. Unfortunately for Amilia, it's right onto her. I thought Tommy had lost it, but when Amilia starts, I see my life flash before my eyes. It's been a pretty fun life, and I'm not ready for it to end. I run to Mom.

Hiding behind Mom seems like the safest thing for me to do. The fact that she starts laughing seems to indicate everything is forgiven, so I start to wag my tail. Unfortunately, she's not laughing because she was happy. She's laughing because she's frustrated.

"Andrew Spurgle, I sentence you to ten minutes of Time Out. You will be eligible for parole if you complete five minutes of Time Out on good behavior. You simply must learn to calm down and share, even with baby sisters like Mabel.

"Tommy Squishes, you will serve five minutes of Time Out for attacking your client. I know Andrew can be a bit much sometimes. You must have patience with him. Everyone grows up on their own timetable. He will eventually grow up and be a big boy. Until then, you have to show him *how* to be a big boy.

"Amilia, we thank you for your service to The Court. I do hope that you enjoy your continued retirement. Please see Bailiff Dad for your cookie.

"Mabel Swabbles, you are being awarded the custody of the Kong for the day. You will lose all ownership rights after bedtime. For the day, though, you can play with the Kong until you are done. At which time, you may hand off the Kong to whomever you wish to.

"Court is dismissed." Judge Mom handed down the sentences quickly, not giving anyone the opportunity to argue. I watch forlornly as Amilia and Mabel practically dance out of the room. Tommy and I follow Mom to our Time Out beds and laid down. Ten Minutes—it might as well be ten years. I'll just close my eyes and hope the time goes by quickly.

An age later, I wake up to someone cuddling next to me. I'm in Time Out. No one should be snuggling me. When I open my eyes, I realize that I slept right through the end of Time Out. The person cuddling me is none other than little Mabel, and she brings a peace offering: the Kong.

"I know you really want this for your museum. I am done playing with it for now. If you want, and you promise to let me play with it sometimes, you can hold it in your museum for safekeeping," Mabel offers.

Bless her little puppy heart. She really is such a good little girl. I graciously accept her offer, resting my head on her shoulders while she takes a nap, the Kong nestled between us.

Love & A Bit of Disorder

Elaine Canyon

Noise from the barn this early in the morning always meant the workday would not be a pleasant one.

Cynthia Lathem stared at the old barn. Most mornings, it was a quiet place, but currently muffled whinnying reached her ears. What had woken them up so early?

She moved up the path to the door, wondering if the griffins and pegasuses were arguing. They always ended up eating out of each other's troughs, and if they woke up early, they'd likely be hungry enough to cause problems.

Old Grant kept them in slapdash pens as opposed to full stalls. He'd inherited the animals and had no idea what to do with them. That was how Cynthia ended up here six months ago. Grant needed someone who knew how to care for his new animals, and Cynthia needed out of her hometown as quickly as possible.

A yell joined the whinnying, followed by crashing and squawking, creating a cacophony.

Panicked, Cynthia ran the last few steps to the door and yanked it open, knocking her bag from her shoulder to her elbow.

Not a single pen still stood. Griffins and pegasuses flew around the tall ceiling in panic, crashing against the walls and into each other.

"Cynthia!"

Cynthia turned to the voice and groaned.

Andrew Spurgle, the new stablehand, clung to the neck of a pegasus fifteen feet in the air. The pegasus, Henry, by the looks of it, was doing everything in his power to throw Andrew off.

"Andrew! What did you do?" Cynthia yelled.

He couldn't respond as Henry turned in a tight circle, almost throwing Andrew to the ground. Her heart stopped for a moment before Andrew righted himself on Henry's back.

"I can explain!" He cut off with a yelp as Henry flew in a loop, thankfully not throwing Andrew down to the rubble below.

For a heartbeat, Cynthia considered ducking back out of the barn and pretending she hadn't shown up to work. Andrew trailed chaos around with him like a security blanket. Cynthia had initially found it endearing, but she wasn't sure she wanted to deal with it today.

An ear-piercing screech cut through her thoughts.

Sandy.

Cynthia scrambled over downed boards to her favorite griffin's pen—well, where it would be if the pens were still standing.

She skidded to a stop next to Sandy, dropping to her knees as her heart skipped a beat and her bag fell to the ground beside her. The big griffin thrashed beneath the debris, her head sticking out among several broken boards, one wing trapped between two boards still connected to a down post. Mud splattered the golden-brown feathers of her face, likely from one of the water troughs spilling during the chaos.

Of all the griffins to get caught in the debris, why did it have to be Sandy? Cynthia was so close to bringing her home. One more month and she'd have enough to buy her. If Andrew was the reason she lost out on Sandy, Cynthia might demand Grant fire him, no matter how much she liked the man.

Sandy screeched and struggled again, the debris shifting, but not enough to free her massive wing. Cynthia brushed the mud from Sandy's face, rubbing soothing circles along her feathers, trying to calm herself as much as the griffin.

"It's all right, girl. I'm here, I'll get you out." She moved the broken boards before gripping the splintering wooden plank that trapped the griffin's wing.

And was immediately knocked flat on her back by a falling stablehand.

Cynthia swore, shoving Andrew off her as she rubbed at where a board had jabbed into her shoulder.

"Sorry!" He jumped up, his legs twisting between the boards she'd moved before falling back onto the dirt, crying out in pain.

Cynthia ignored the concern rising in her chest. Sandy might be hurt and couldn't be healed in the same way as Andrew. Besides, if Cynthia had learned anything in the last month of Andrew working here, this debacle was his doing.

"Hold on, I'll help you in a minute." She turned from him and gripped the wooden plank again, heaving as she slowly lifted it high enough for Sandy to free her wing. Sandy stood and stretched her long wings out, moving them in a circular motion. Then she took to the air. The griffin flew a tight loop around the ceiling, knocking against another griffin, before landing near an overturned grain trough with a proud shake of her head. Cynthia took a moment to enjoy the relief that washed over her before looking back to the chaos.

Time to heal Andrew.

Cynthia turned to where he sat on the ground. Andrew held his ankle close against him, sucking air in through his clenched teeth.

"Let's see it." Cynthia found her bag, praying she had everything to ask Mother Land to fix his ankle.

Of the Three Sisters, creators of the world and all its creatures, Cynthia appreciated she'd been born a human, a child of the Land. Mother Land loved all her children—including Andrew, a quiet voice reminded her—and with the right training, any human could call on Mother Land for a variety of things. Cynthia smiled as she undid the latch. Mother Land wasn't the only one who saw things to enjoy in Andrew.

Andrew released his ankle, then hissed and pulled it back into him. "No, I'll just hold on to it."

"It'll be all right, we'll get you fixed up." Cynthia threw open her bag and pulled out her candle. "But what on earth did you do? Did you try to take Henry for a fly?"

"No!" Andrew let go of his ankle and reached for her, only to grab it again with a yelp. "I can explain! You see, what happened was I accidentally let Henry out of his pen." He glanced up at the pegasus he'd been hanging from when she'd walked in, then snapped his gaze back to her. "And I couldn't coax him back in. So, I thought I'd get a lead on Mavis, since Henry likes to be around Mavis and use her as bait to get him back in the pen. Then Mavis got it in her head we were going outside, and while I tried to get control of her, Henry started in on it, and next thing I knew, the pens were crashing down and all of them were flying and then I was in the air with Henry and then you walked in."

Andrew gulped in air and Cynthia forced her smile down with the reminder he could have killed Sandy. Only Andrew could demolish the interior of a barn in less than a minute.

"He would have gone back in on his own." She sighed. "We've talked about this. They aren't horses. Stop thinking of them that way."

Cynthia tore the corner off a letter for her mother. The invitation for her parents to visit in the next few days wouldn't work out if she didn't fix this mess first. She set the torn corner next to the candle. White for bone. Now she needed something red.

"Here." Andrew pushed his hand into her vision, dropping a mess of squashed berries next to her candle on the ground. "They were my breakfast before all this."

Cynthia gaped at him. "Why didn't you use the berries to coax Henry back into his pen?"

"Why would I do that?" Andrew wiped his hand on his pant leg with a grimace before returning it to where his other hand still gripped his ankle.

"Because pegasuses love berries." Cynthia couldn't believe he'd had berries all along and hadn't bothered to even try.

When Grant told her about hiring Andrew, Cynthia thought it would be fun to teach someone all about caring for griffins and pegasuses, especially considering his experience with horses. The extra help during the day was an added benefit. The last month with Andrew hadn't given her as much help as she'd hoped, but Andrew was good company, even if things had a habit of spiraling out of control around him.

Andrew's face blossomed as red as the berries.

"I didn't know that." He dropped his head against his knee and clenched his jaw.

Cynthia's eyes traced the hard line from his jaw into his brown hair, tousled from the chaos, then back to his chin. Maybe Mother Land went out of her way to make him good-looking to help compensate for how he carried havoc in his back pocket.

Sandy nudged Cynthia's arm aside, startling her from admiring Andrew's physique, and rummaged in the bag.

"Hurry and eat it before they see you." Cynthia blew her black fringe from her eyes. Sandy started pulling out the stone fruit in Cynthia's bag. Grant didn't approve of the sugar, but Sandy was almost hers. She was counting on the stone fruit to help ease Sandy's transition from Grant's stable.

"Why do you bring her treats?" Andrew looked up from his knee.

"Let's fix your ankle." Cynthia pulled out her matches and lit the candle, evading Andrew's question. For someone so out of control, she didn't expect him to have noticed that she'd snuck Sandy fruit every morning. She set the candle next to his ankle. "Try to stay still so the smoke can get to you."

He braced himself against her side, and she ignored how firm his arm was against hers.

Cynthia lit the candle, then the scrap of paper, and set it on top of the berries. "White for bone. Red for blood. Mother Land, we beg thy healing for thy son."

The smoke turned pure white as it burned through the paper. Tendrils of smoke circled Andrew's ankle. The wet berries caught fire as quickly as dry grass, sending red smoke to join the white.

Andrew yelled in pain, tipping into the ground away from her. Cynthia rushed to pull him back up and against her side, worried his leg would leave the healing smoke.

"It'll be over in a moment." She tried to prop him up and rest his head on her shoulder, but Andrew was stouter than she expected. Fighting against his weight, she settled with him half-propped against her side, and his head resting on her chest. He smelled of the barn, but the faintest scent of a forest walk pushed through. Did he always smell this good? His cold sweat dampened her shirt, and she realized she should probably try again to prop him up against her shoulder rather than letting him keep his face in her chest. She shifted to move him, but he cried out and Cynthia froze, afraid to cause more pain. It would be fine. It wasn't like they were involved or anything. She was just supporting a work friend with a very broken ankle by letting him rest his face against her chest. And she definitely was not affected by his warm breath against her...

She needed to focus. He needed help; she was there to provide it. She could do this.

"Healing often hurts more than breaking does, but it's better than living with the pain." Cynthia hesitated a moment before rubbing her hand against his back.

"Easy for you to say," he ground out through haggard breaths.

Fair. She wasn't the one Mother Land was healing. But she had been before.

"I was ten. I fell from a tree and broke my arm. When my parents got everything together to heal me, I thought my mama had messed up the prayer and Mother Land was breaking my arm more. My papa had to hold me down so that I'd stop moving away from the smoke."

Andrew let out a low chuckle, cut short by a sharp hiss and a loud pop from his ankle. Cynthia tightened her grip on him as he slumped against her. The white smoke disappeared as the paper turned to ash. The last of the berries still twirled red smoke around his ankle.

"You're almost there. Just think, once your ankle is better, you can help me fix all this before Grant checks on us."

He barked a laugh, and Cynthia chuckled. Andrew was a chaotic mess of a man, but he was a fun chaotic mess—broken pens notwithstanding.

The berries were nothing but black ash now as the last tendrils of red smoke faded into the air and the candle snuffed out. Andrew let out a shuddering sigh, his hot breath wafting across her chest as he turned further into her. Cynthia's face heated. They were far too close, and if Grant walked in and saw Andrew's face pressed against her chest on top of the mess, they'd both likely lose their jobs.

"Come on." She gave into a secret desire and grabbed his hair, tugging loosely on the damp, silky strands. Was his hair always this soft, or was it just today? "This mess needs to be cleaned up."

Andrew's head followed her hand up from her chest, chasing it the way the barn cats did when Cynthia took time to pet them. She dropped her hand to the ground, and he followed it for a moment before snapping upright.

"Thank you." Andrew cleared his throat and looked down at his ankle, his face falling with a dejected sigh. "And I'm sorry about all this. I'm a mess."

Against her better judgment, Cynthia put her hand on his shoulder. "You're new, it happens."

Andrew shook his head, but didn't argue with her. He pushed himself up, hesitating before setting his weight on his healed ankle. "Well, at least that went right today." He smiled and offered her his hand.

Cynthia let him lift her up, enjoying how his callouses rubbed against her own when he slipped his fingers from hers. "More will go right today, you'll see."

"If it does, it'll be all your fault, believe me." He looked around the barn. "I guess first we need new pens to put them in?"

Cynthia wished she could pull the dejected look off his face. Scowling didn't suit Andrew, especially when that scowl was likely accompanied with aggravation at himself. As much as he was chaos embodied, Cynthia liked Andrew. She could do without the problems that followed him around, and based on his face, he could, too.

"Let's grab tools from the workshop and see if there's any spare wood and nails before Grant finds all this. Not all these boards are usable." She reached for him, hoping to bring his smile back, but Sandy's head intercepted her hand. Cynthia blinked at the annoyance that hit her, then shook it off. "Don't worry, girl. Andrew and I will get your bed back together." She scratched beneath Sandy's feathers, eliciting a loud purr. "Be good." Cynthia kissed Sandy's head and moved to the door.

Andrew followed her out into the crisp morning air. Cynthia started to reach for him again, but he stuck both hands deep in his pockets and didn't look at her. He didn't want her comfort.

Or, more likely, her pity.

Cynthia thought back to how she'd seen Grant and his wife, Jane, interact with Andrew. They laced pity into everything they said and did regarding Andrew. Earlier that week, she'd overheard Grant telling a neighbor he'd hired Andrew because the man was going to end up without a roof over his head if someone didn't give him a chance. Cynthia understood what Grant meant. If the last month was any indication, Andrew brought chaos into all parts of his life. But he also brought a lot of fun, and his debacles aside, Andrew had a knack for griffins.

That counted for something in Cynthia's book.

She let it be quiet as they walked the well-worn path to Grant's workshop, but as they approached the building, Cynthia couldn't take his silence any longer.

"I know pegasuses aren't your thing." She bumped his shoulder with hers and his mouth tilted up ever so slightly to the left. A win. "But you're good with the griffins. Have you worked with them before?"

"Nah, but they're just big cats, and I'm good with cats."

"I don't think I'd call a griffin a cat."

"The eagle head and wings are different, sure, but they act like cats." Andrew opened the door for her and followed her into the workshop. "You had Sandy purring before we left the barn. They're more like cats than they are birds. I bet I could get one to play with a big ball of yarn."

"I might pay to see that," Cynthia laughed as they walked up to the workbench. "Just please don't do it inside the barn."

Andrew rolled his eyes but smiled at her. Another win. Smiling-Andrew was much better than grumpy-mad-at-himself-Andrew.

The morning light from the windows above the workbench gave his hair a rusty look, and Cynthia had to turn away to keep from staring. The pieces of farming equipment around the large building were far less appealing, but much safer to look at. Andrew cleared his throat, and she spun back to face him.

"Looks like Grant has enough nails." He picked up a bucket from the workbench and gestured to the four still there. His arm swung back to his side and knocked several odds and ends on the bench to the floor. Andrew stooped to pick them up and dumped half his bucket of nails.

"Stop, stop." Cynthia pressed her lips together to keep from laughing. "Set the bucket down and I'll help you get the nails cleaned up."

Andrew sighed as he set the bucket of nails down on the worn wooden floor.

She grabbed the old broom by the door and pushed all the nails into one pile while Andrew picked up the assorted items he'd knocked from the workbench.

"There. Now it'll be easier to get the nails cleaned up." She knelt on the floor, scooping up handfuls of nails and dropping them in the bucket, Andrew following along after her.

"See, it's like it never happened." Cynthia smiled at him, but Andrew's returning grin looked forced.

"Like I said, anything good today is your fault." His eyes bore into hers, and Cynthia wondered if he'd let her get lost there for a few hours.

She looked away, desperate for something for her hands to do. She stood and grabbed two hammers from where they hung on the wall and changed the subject. "Nails, hammers, and now to see if there's any scrap wood."

The door opened, and the one voice Cynthia didn't want to hear until they'd fixed the barn sounded behind her.

"What do you need scrap wood for, Cynthia?"

Cynthia tried not to cringe as she turned to face Grant.

Andrew cleared his throat. "We need to—"

"We need to fix a hole in Henry's stall." Cynthia cut him off. "He kicked out a board between Mavis's pen and his."

Her heart beat in her ears while she watched Grant mull over her lie. Finally, he shook his head, raking his fingers through his thinning gray hair.

"I hate to move any of them, but if he's this bent on Mavis, I don't see any other choice. Switch him around so he's not near her. I bought all the cut wood when my neighbor passed; there's plenty to spare. It's behind the workshop."

"We'll take care of it." Cynthia hoped her voice sounded calmer than she felt. What if Grant asked to see the damage? What if he stopped by the barn before they'd finished fixing the pens?

"I'm heading out for the day," Grant said, and Cynthia hoped he was unaware of her pounding heart. "Jane wants to visit the grandchildren and I've put her off too long already. Will you be all right without me?"

"We'll be fine, right, Andrew?" She looked over at Andrew so she wouldn't need to keep looking at Grant. The softest smile she'd ever seen spread across his face.

"Don't worry about us. Cynthia has everything under control."

Grant nodded. "I won't be back before you leave for the day, so I'll see you tomorrow."

Cynthia nodded, holding her breath as Grant turned and headed out the door. She counted twenty heartbeats before releasing her breath in a whoosh.

"Now we know where to get the wood." She looked back at Andrew, that soft smile still on his face.

"Why did you lie for me?"

She opened her mouth, but her throat went tight and her mouth dry. A strangled hum was all she managed.

"Sorry." Andrew's smile fell, and he grabbed the back of his neck. "You don't need to tell me; just thanks. I thought I'd lost my job there for a moment."

Cynthia nodded and swallowed, her throat still too tight to speak. And because she didn't know what else to do, she led them out of the workshop.

They dropped the tools and nails off at the barn before Cynthia led them back to get the wood. Grant's neighbor must have been planning to build another building before he died. Cynthia wished they could build proper stalls, but if they did, Grant would know something more than a broken board happened. He'd likely fire Andrew for it, and Cynthia wasn't having that. Yes, she and Andrew weren't on the best of terms at the moment. Tension permeated everything they were doing. But it was her fault, not Andrew's.

Why hadn't she answered him?

It wasn't a big deal.

They were friends, and friends watched out for each other.

At least, she thought they were friends.

"Can I ask you something?" She kept her eyes down on the wood plank they carried.

"Sure."

"Are we friends?"

Andrew didn't answer for a long time, and Cynthia tried to ignore the disappointment that filled her chest. She should have known better.

They set the plank down on top of the rest of the pieces they'd carried to the barn.

"I want to be friends."

It took two heartbeats for Cynthia to process what Andrew had said.

"I thought we were friends." She chanced a glance at him, missing his soft smile from before. "That was why I lied to Grant. Friends look out for each other."

Andrew reached for her, linking their hands and sending a shiver down her back. "I'm sorry. We are friends. I just didn't think someone as competent as you would want to be friends with someone like me."

Cynthia gripped his hand before he could let her go. "You're too hard on yourself."

He shrugged, but that soft smile pulled on his lips again, and Cynthia's chest warmed.

"Let's go get another set of boards." He held onto her hand as he turned.

And fell facefirst over the stack of wood, pulling Cynthia down to the ground with him.

"Sorry!" Andrew pushed up from the woodpile, only to lose his balance and crash to the ground—again.

The pile scattered beneath him, one plank smacking Cynthia's shoulder. Pain shot through her and she curled in on herself. She really needed to keep Andrew away from things like precariously stacked piles of wood, if for no other reason than her personal safety.

"I'm sorry." Andrew groaned again and swore under his breath.

Cynthia turned to where Andrew laid sprawled out on the ground. She sighed. A part of her wanted to be mad at him, but the dejected look on his face cut through her anger. Yes, her shoulder stung, but probably not as sharply as Andrew's embarrassment.

"It's all right." She shifted away from the wood before standing.

Andrew stayed sprawled on the ground, staring up at the blue sky above them.

"Really, it's all right." Cynthia moved to him and held out her hand. "It happens."

"More to me than anyone."

Cynthia frowned at his forlorn face. This was getting ridiculous. So he embodied chaos. That didn't mean he needed to mope over it. Besides, he said they were friends, and friends pulled each other out of their slumps.

"Enough." She reached down and grabbed his wrist, yanking to pull him to a sitting position. "Andrew Spurgle, I refuse to sit here and let you wallow in self-pity. Your life is what it is, and amazingly enough, people like you for you, even if you bring a bit of disorder into the world."

He shook his head, his gaze now fixed on the ground. "That's exactly why people don't like me."

"I like you." Cynthia rested her fists on her hips. "Doesn't that count for something?"

Andrew looked up at her, his eyes tracing from her black hair down to her brown boots. Cynthia's body buzzed as his eyes took her in, that soft smile tugging on his lips.

"It does." His whisper sent heat coursing through her body, and Cynthia swallowed hard against it.

"Well, good." She forced her eyes away from him, trying to calm her soaring heartbeat. "Let's get the rest of the wood."

Andrew stood and nodded. She chanced a glance at him and noticed that soft smile had graced his lips again. Cynthia pulled her eyes away. It was one thing to be his friend, but she realized her heart was pushing past friends with Andrew. That was a recipe for her own kind of chaos. It was the same chaos that drove her half a day's journey from home.

What else was she supposed to do? She had summoned the courage to tell the man she'd been with for months that she loved him, and he'd not only told her she was crazy, but spread the rumor through the entire town that she'd been unfaithful.

Best just be Andrew's friend until she knew if he was interested in her that way or not.

Unless he made the first move, Cynthia would play it safe.

They set the last of the wood down near the barn, and Andrew swallowed hard as Cynthia smiled at him.

He had to be reading her wrong. But the way her cheeks bloomed pink every time she caught him staring had built a strange emotion in his chest.

Hope.

"Well, there's no putting this off now." Cynthia turned to the barn, her black braid swinging against her back. "Are you ready?"

"You tell me what to do. I'll try to not make a bigger mess."

She rolled her gold eyes at him, but bit her lip as she grinned. Andrew rubbed the back of his neck, trying to think of something, anything, to say that might sweep her off her feet. He wanted her to see him as more than a buffoon. Most people knew he was a buffoon, but he yearned for Cynthia to see him as something more, something better.

"You're ridiculous." She grabbed the barn door. "Let's get started."

He followed her into the barn and groaned at the mess he'd made. At least the animals were all back on the ground, but the debris from the pens looked even worse now that the pegasuses and griffins had been walking and lying on it.

"We've got this." Cynthia patted his arm and his skin tingled for a brief second. "Let's start with the pegasuses' side. They're more flighty than the griffins."

He knew that all too well now. "I can move the debris off to the side if you can help get the pegasuses out of the way. It's probably best that I give them some space."

"At least Henry and Mavis." She bumped his shoulder with his, leaning into him. Andrew summoned some courage and shifted to wrap his arm around her, agonizing over if it was the right move. Then his arm hit feathers.

"Hello, Sandy." He sighed and settled for scratching the griffin's head. "Sorry about all this."

Sandy pushed into his hand and stepped between him and Cynthia.

"Don't worry, girl. Andrew and I are going to put everything right." Cynthia wrapped her arms around Sandy's neck, her fingers brushing against his. He swallowed, moving to take her hand, but she shifted to secure Sandy in a halter.

Andrew pushed down the disappointment and stepped back so Cynthia could begin securing animals and started in on clearing the debris. There would be other chances to hold her hand. At least, he hoped there would be.

There was enough wood to build full stalls for them. He was glad that had gone right. Cynthia talked all the time about how the animals needed real stalls, and now she could build what they needed. Just as soon as he got this mess cleared up.

The first plank of wood he grabbed gave him a splinter. Great.

Please, Mother Land, don't let it be a sign.

Despite his initial concern, the steady movement of clearing debris calmed his mind. The cacophony that always played in his head muffled a small amount as he focused on picking up the scattered boards of wood. Sweat dripped down his back as he picked up his pace. His speed, while soothing, caused his shirt to catch on the jagged edge of a board. Andrew huffed at the sound of fabric tearing. He hated mending clothes. His fingers always ended up with more holes in them than the item he was sewing. Hoping to cut down on the bleeding he'd be doing tonight, Andrew pulled his shirt over his head.

He froze at the small sound of Cynthia's gasp.

Fearing she'd hurt herself, he spun to find her staring at him. Her face was as red as the berries he'd been eating for breakfast, her eyes wide, and her mouth agape.

"Are you all right?" His own face heated. Taking his shirt off was a bad idea. He'd made her uncomfortable; embarrassed her and now himself. He was a fool. Why had he thought there was anything there? Obviously, there wasn't.

Black blocked out all but a thin band of gold in her beautiful eyes as she stared back at him. After an excruciating moment, she nodded.

"Sorry." She looked down and some of the color drained from her face. "You're doing a good job. Once you get the last corner cleared up, we'll be ready to build the stalls."

"Right." Andrew frowned as Cynthia looked everywhere but at him. He was already embarrassed beyond his norm. Why stop now? "I can put my shirt back on."

"No!" Cynthia's eyes shot up to look at him, her face flooded with her blush, deeper than it had been before. "I mean, you don't have to. I...I know it's hot work. If you need it off, it's...it's fine."

Maybe he hadn't been reading things wrong? He'd be risking making a fool of himself, but he'd been doing that all day—all month, if he was honest. There was nothing left to lose, and Cynthia to gain. Andrew determined to play all in for a chance with the beautiful stablehand in front of him.

He smiled. "Well, tell me if it bothers you, all right?"

Cynthia bit her lip as her blush deepened and nodded.

Clearing the debris gained a new purpose as Andrew worked, taking the time to arrange the wood into piles of what he thought was still usable and what needed to end up behind Grant's workshop. He only tripped twice and ended up with three more splinters. Andrew didn't notice it all that much, at least not with Cynthia glancing at him every few minutes, a shy smile gracing her pretty mouth.

"This is excellent." She came up behind him as he finished sorting the last of the debris.

Andrew wiped his brow on the back of his arm. "You must be rubbing off on me."

Another of her smiles rewarded him. Grant could pay him in her smiles, and Andrew wouldn't complain. Actually, that might be all he got paid in once he told Grant the truth. Knowing the likelihood that he wouldn't see Cynthia everyday after this left a bitter taste in his mouth. He grabbed a hammer to distract him from his gloomy thoughts, but his hand didn't cooperate as he dropped it on top of the pile of mostly usable pieces.

"At least it wasn't my foot." Andrew huffed and picked up the hammer, embarrassment burning hot in his gut. But he was playing all in for a chance with Cynthia, and that meant pushing off the embarrassment and mishaps.

Cynthia slipped her hand around his left bicep, and Andrew stopped breathing as his skin exploded with the same tingling he'd previewed earlier. This had to be what it would feel like to pick up the flame from a candle. Touching raw light had to feel like Cynthia touching his skin.

"I'm glad it didn't hit your foot. I don't want to sacrifice my entire letter to heal you multiple times."

"Your letter?" Andrew silently cursed at how his voice had come out so small.

"I tore the corner off a letter to my parents to heal you before." Her fingers slid down the length of his arm before she let go of him.

His ability to think returned, but Andrew would have given up the clarity of mind to keep her hand on his skin. He cleared his throat and thought back to what she'd said.

"Do your parents not live close by?"

"They're about half a day south of here." Cynthia picked up her hammer, using it to point at several boards that had come through the chaos in decent shape. "Let's start with Henry's pen in the back."

"Did this job bring you out here?" Andrew helped her pick up the stack of boards.

"Sort of." Her voice went tight, and he kicked himself for opening up a touchy topic.

"What do we need to do for the stalls you want?" He changed the subject.

"We can't build the stalls I want. We have to build the pens just as they were." They set the boards down near the wall, and she turned to look at him with her hands on her hips. The exasperated look on her face should have left him feeling foolish, but this time, it emboldened him.

"And why not?" He mirrored her stance.

"Because Grant will know there was more damage than just a broken board in Henry's pen." She gestured around the barn.

"I have to tell him the truth, anyway." Andrew shrugged. "We might as well sweeten the deal for him by improving what we can."

She stepped up to him and grabbed his arm. "You can't tell Grant the truth! I lied so he wouldn't fire you!"

The fire she sent through his arm made it hard to think, but Andrew held on to his resolve with a death grip. "I will not make you a liar, Cynthia, especially not for me. You deserve better than that; you are better than that. Don't worry, I've been fired before. It's not the greatest feeling, but I usually figure something out."

Her panicked stare softened in her eyes, pulling him closer. He might as well have been a harnessed griffin with Cynthia holding the lead.

Until he smacked his forehead against hers.

"Sorry!" Andrew grimaced as pain splintered along his skull.

She laughed and rubbed her forehead as she looked up at him. "You're set on this, then? We really don't have to tell him."

"I have to tell him." He reached for her, tucking a stray lock from her braid behind her ear. "Build the stalls with me, Cynthia. Then if Grant fires me, at least I know you got the stalls you wanted."

The fight in her eyes softened and her shoulders fell with a long sigh. "All right, fine. If you're going to tell him what happened, anyway, let's make sure these stalls are as good as we can make them. It'll be a lot harder to see you if you don't work here."

"Harder to see me?" He must have hit his head with more force than he thought. That or he hit her head too hard and rattled her intelligence.

"If you still wanted to see me." She bit her lip as she grinned, and her gold eyes stared up at him.

"I would." He barely heard his own voice over the rushing of blood in his ears.

They stared at each other, Andrew's heart beating to the same rhythm as the dull waves of pain radiating across his forehead.

"All right." Cynthia looked over at where she'd tethered all the griffins and pegasuses. "Let's get to it. We'll spin this in the best light so Grant won't fire you."

"How are you going to spin this in a good light?" Andrew laughed. If she didn't stop saying things like this, he was going to fall head over heels for her, hopefully just figuratively. He'd hit his head enough today.

"You realized we could use some of the wood he bought for building stalls. Your technique for pulling all the pens down was questionable, but the results are admirable." Cynthia said it so matter-of-factly, Andrew almost believed it himself.

She was too good to be true.

"Show me what to do." He picked up a board. She didn't need to know right now he'd still tell Grant the truth of what happened.

Right now, she could keep looking at him like he was worth the fight.

And she did, for the rest of the afternoon and into the night as they built stalls together. By the time they finished, Andrew hoped maybe Cynthia was right and Grant wouldn't fire him.

The oil lamp near the door cast long shadows through the barn as they led Sandy into her new stall. The other animals had already settled in. Andrew determined Cynthia needed her own barn full of griffins for how much the animals liked their new spaces.

Sandy immediately climbed onto the platform in the center of her stall. Cynthia had them build a perch for each animal. The new stalls took up more room than the pens had. It made maneuvering in the barn a little tight, but Andrew figured the griffins and pegasuses needed the space more than the human caretakers. Sandy squawked, turning around once before settling down on the platform and preening one of her wings.

Cynthia jumped, grabbing onto the ledge and heaving herself up onto the platform. She barely fit up against Sandy's side, but the griffin happily tucked Cynthia under her wing.

"I'll build you a big platform like this when I bring you home." She snuggled into the fur on Sandy's back.

"Bring her home?" Andrew smiled up at Cynthia, cuddled against the massive griffin.

"Next month, I'll have enough to buy her. I've been saving every scrap to bring her home since I got the shed in my garden fixed up."

"That's why you bring her treats." Andrew rested his arms on the gate, only to have it swing out, then back, and smack him. He sighed and latched the gate closed before testing his weight against it again. At least it hadn't smacked Cynthia, too.

"The woman who taught me to look after griffins told me the fastest way to their hearts was through stone fruit. Once I finished building a place for Sandy at my house, I started bringing her preserved stone fruit every day. Since they're in season now, she gets fresh ones." When he'd asked about the fruit that morning, she'd avoided the topic, but now she smiled at him, looking pleased he'd asked.

"And when you buy her, she'll have all the stone fruit she wants." Andrew chuckled, then gave her a teasing grin. "I can't believe you're going to take Sandy from me."

Cynthia rolled her eyes at him. "If you're nice to me, maybe I'll let you visit her."

Heat flooded him as his heart doubled its beat. Andrew took a steadying breath, fighting his mind's attempt to spin out of control from her words. She'd been doing that all afternoon and evening. Saying little things that twisted his chest and made him hope she might accept if he asked for more than friendship from her.

But he still didn't know how to ask.

"I'll start with putting the tools away." He spun, hoping to buy himself some time, then knocked over an empty nail bucket. Andrew scooped it up along with both hammers, the saws, and two other empty buckets.

"Careful," Cynthia called as he stumbled out the door, not quite dropping all the items in his arms.

The chilly night air cleared his mind, and he realized as he stepped out into the dark, he'd made a fool of himself again. He had no light. Andrew wasn't about to go back into the barn until he had a plan. He refused to let the regular chaos that followed him tirelessly ruin his chance with Cynthia.

Slow steps led him further down the well-worn path to the workshop. He didn't bother to reposition the buckets blocking his view, reasoning there was no point with the moon and stars as his only light. He would go slow and find a candle at the workshop. Everything was fine.

At least until a divot in the ground sent him sprawling, leaving his face pressed into the dirt.

"Who's there?"

Andrew groaned. Of course Grant would be out here. At least Andrew had his shirt back on. Grant was definitely not who he wanted to impress that way. Andrew pushed up to sitting, feeling the sting of a scrape on his wrist. Maybe it would help distract from the blow when Grant fired him.

"It's me, Grant, didn't mean to spook you." He looked up and saw a small light a short way off, illuminating Grant's stout form.

"What are you still doing here?"

No sense in putting off the inevitable. Andrew stood up and faced Grant as he came closer. "I let Cynthia cover for me this morning. Henry did more than break a board. I made a mistake and caused all the animals to break down their pens. Cynthia and I have just finished building new stalls for them."

Andrew waited for Grant to say it, to tell him not to come back tomorrow, but Grant was silent as he studied him. Andrew squirmed. The past employers who had raged at him were easier to handle than Grant's scrutinizing silence.

"I'll get these things put away." Andrew stooped to collect everything he'd dropped. He stacked the three buckets and put as many of the tools that would fit in the top one. The extra time it took rewarded him with a free hand, and the ability to see where he was going. Maybe when he tripped again, he could catch himself.

"You'll need to be on time tomorrow." Grant handed Andrew the candlestick.

Grant's words echoed three times in Andrew's mind before he comprehended them. Warmth flooded his chest, and his throat constricted.

He wasn't fired.

He'd been so sure of it, sure that there was no coming back from this. That it would be time to move on and find someone else willing to pay him for a month or so before they fired him, too.

Without Cynthia's help, that's exactly what would have happened.

"Right." Andrew adjusted his grip on the candlestick, keeping the dripping wax from burning his hand. "You should go look at what Cynthia did. The stalls are amazing and she made some smart improvements to the barn."

"I don't doubt that." Grant cracked a grin. "And you know if you hurt Cynthia, I will fire you, right?"

Andrew's heart stuttered to a stop before picking back up with a speed that flooded his ears. Was this what it was like meeting a woman's father? He'd never had a woman willing to stick around him long enough to get that far. But he wanted to reassure Grant, wanted to let him know he'd make the effort both with Cynthia and on the farm.

"I'd fire me, too." Andrew met Grant's stare.

"I knew you were a good pick. I'll stop in and assure Cynthia I'm not firing you. And then you make sure she gets home all right." Grant's smile shifted to a smirk. "Just to her door. She can handle the rest of it without you."

Andrew's jaw fell to his boots before he yanked it back up. What in Mother Land's name was he supposed to say to that? He settled for a quick nod. "Got it."

Grant patted his shoulder before walking past him.

Andrew didn't waste any time in making his way to the workshop and getting everything put away. By the time Andrew made it back to the barn, Grant was on his way out.

"Thanks for this." Andrew handed him back the candle.

"You're welcome. And you were right: Cynthia knows what she's doing. Those stalls will be the talk of the farmers once I've shown them off to everyone."

"She's something special." Andrew looked past Grant to the barn. He wasn't sure which was more nerve-wracking, telling Grant the truth a few minutes ago, or knowing he was about to ask Cynthia if he could walk her home.

"You've got this. We'll see you tomorrow." Grant patted his shoulder again before heading into the dark.

Andrew took a moment, trying to decide how to broach the subject of walking Cynthia home. He didn't think she'd oppose the idea, but he'd been nothing but a buffoon the entire day—frankly, the whole month he'd worked with her—and he just wanted to be normal for one minute with her.

"Why are you out here? It's so cold."

Andrew jumped at Cynthia's voice as she joined him in the cold night air.

"I was about to come in." He smiled as she stepped against him. He could do this. Slowly, he shifted his arm, sliding it up her back so that no griffins could interfere, until it rested on her shoulders.

Cynthia went still for a heart-stopping moment before curling into him and Andrew's heart shuddered back to life. Emboldened, he rested his head against her hair to whisper in her ear.

"May I walk you home?"

He felt her sharp intake of breath and held his own as he waited for an answer.

"Grant told me I could take Sandy home today, and tomorrow pay him what I have for her." She tilted her head towards him, bringing their lips dangerously close. "Would you like us to fly you home?"

"Then I won't know that you made it home all right." Andrew pulled her closer, shifting so their foreheads could rest against each other. "Let's get Sandy settled in, and I'll walk home."

"You could sleep in the shed with Sandy." She smirked at him, teasing shining in her gold eyes.

"Tempting." He grinned and tucked a loose strand of hair behind her ear. "So tempting."

"Andrew?" Her tongue darted out, wetting her lips.

Enthralled by the action, Andrew almost forgot to respond. "Cynthia?"

"If you're going to kiss me, please don't smack my head again."

He laughed, relief washing through him. He'd not read her wrong after all. "You're fine if I kiss you, then?"

"If you don't, I might lose my mind." Her hands tightened on his shirt, pulling him closer.

"I lose enough stuff for the two of us." Andrew wrapped his arms around her, bringing his lips to hers in a slow slide as she melted against him.

And the noise in his head went silent, replaced by Cynthia's quiet sigh as he kissed her under the stars.

Lead The Way

TC Ross

Grass stains mixed with mud and blood covered Princess Zanna's tunic and leather leggings. A few twigs stuck out of her messy brown hair. She glided past several young Fae playing with rabbits around the rim of the cistern that hid their subterranean castle. They gaped, their eyes locked on her and her husband.

A moment later, she landed in the courtyard at the top of the castle. The guards cringed away, clenching their fists at their sides. It was a testament to their training that they didn't pinch their noses to avoid the stench she'd had hours to grow accustomed to.

"Princess Zanna. Aeron..." Jude, the head guard, trailed off, speechless, as his nose wrinkled. He fanned his fuzzy lime-green wings, clearing the air in his immediate vicinity.

"I need the scouts and guards called up to begin a search that may go outside the kingdom." Zanna flicked her wings. Dirt flaked off, revealing the orange and black patterning beneath.

"At once," added Aeron, baring his pointed teeth. His night blue dragonfly wings rasped against each other.

"Do you need a healer?" Jude asked, a deeply concerned look darkening his countenance.

"No. It's just scratches." Zanna dragged a hand over her arm, peeling off a layer of dried mud. "Jude, you're not moving."

"Pardon, Your Highness, but the king and queen gave us orders not to honor your requests for guard action without going through the proper channels."

"Proper channels?" She raised an eyebrow at the much taller man.

"Yes. Why do you need the scouts and guards?" Jude shifted from one foot to the other.

Zanna flared her wings, her boots hitting the stone with ominous thuds. She rushed into Jude, jabbing a finger into the center of his armored chest. "My son, Prince Asher, could be *lost* somewhere outside the kingdom. That's. What's. Wrong."

Jude stumbled back until he hit the stone wall.

"Dear, we should explain," said Aeron, placing a hand on her shoulder. He pulled her back slowly, carefully, as if she were a rattlesnake ready to strike.

"I'm pretty sure the prince is eating lunch," piped up one of the other guards, bowing to Zanna.

"You've seen him?" She spun so fast that she almost knocked Aeron down with her wings.

"A short time ago, Your Highness. I swear he came through the main doors covered in blackberry juice."

"Really?" snapped Zanna. "We've been out all morning searching for him, and he's *here*?"

"Yes, ma'am."

"You're sure?"

"Yes, ma'am."

"I'm going to kill him!"

"No, you're not." Aeron wrapped an arm over her chest, pinning her wings to her back with his body. "This wasn't entirely his fault."

"He stole a map," protested Zanna. Heat coursed through her body, her rage begging to be unleashed upon the proper target. "Or more likely copied it. I'm still not convinced he stole it. He's too smart for that."

"A map? Ma'am, what exactly happened?" Jude sidestepped to the doorway.

"Spurgle happened," Zanna hissed. "If he hadn't left that map out in the open…if Asher hadn't taken it…"

"Yes, yes, honey-sweet," whispered Aeron. "We're not going inside while you're so upset. He doesn't deserve to be yelled at."

"Oh, doesn't he?"

"What happened?" repeated Jude, glancing over his shoulder into the entry hall. "Should I send for the prince?"

"No," she grumbled reluctantly. Her stomach growled, adding to her list of complaints. Somewhere in the back of her mind, reason spoke. *Calm down. I've had a long day, and Asher is safe.*

"This morning, we were eating breakfast on the main flight balcony," said Aeron, tilting his chin to study the layers of exposed rock overhead. "Spurgle came to talk to us…"

Aeron

The morning sunlight filtered through the bushes, illuminating the far wall as if it were full of diamonds. Clear, clean spring water cascaded over the rocks, ending its journey from within the earth to the pool below.

A variety of Fae, from the water-loving Naiads, his kind, and Parpar, Zanna's butterfly-winged people, filled every balcony. A few Parpar Ash, towering fuzzy-winged guards, moved among them, chatting and enjoying breakfast. Their voices echoed off the limestone walls in a comforting murmur.

"One of the hunting parties brought down a pronghorn antelope last night," said Aeron, spearing a chunk of dark red meat with his fork. "They brought back the liver first. Shame you don't enjoy it like we do."

Zanna grimaced, her suntanned face scrunching up around her nose. "You eat it raw."

"Well, yes. That's the best way to eat it." Aeron made a show of sinking his teeth into the chunk and shearing off a smaller bite.

"I'm sure I'll have some for lunch." Zanna delicately pinched off a piece of the pastry on her plate. "The blackberries are in season."

"Which means it's going to be too hot to leave the colony during the day for the rest of the summer," he said, shuddering.

"For you."

"I will dry out into a scarecrow."

"Don't be so dramatic."

"Easy for you to say, you—"

A commotion drew his eyes to the doors leading inside. The guards stood in the doorway, blocking someone from entering. "I need to speak with Princess Suzanna immediately!"

Aeron said nothing, chewing slowly.

Zanna sipped her tea as if she had heard nothing.

"Princess, I know you can hear me!" persisted Andrew Spurgle, his voice rising with indignation. "Your son stole a valuable map from my collection."

That wasn't like Asher at all.

"I saw him going north. He's going to find the Fairy Circle, and then what are you going to do? How would you find him if he were walking around as a human among them?" Spurgle shouted, trying to look past the towering moth-winged guards. "Don't say I didn't warn you!"

Zanna set her teacup down so hard it cracked the saucer.

"Let him through," said Aeron, meeting her eyes and holding their intense gaze. He lifted a hand, gesturing to the guards.

"I am the wronged party," huffed Spurgle, making a show of straightening his green and gold vest. He raked a hand through a head covered with far too glorious blond waves as he strode across the balcony.

"You're accusing a member of the royal family of theft." Zanna didn't look at him, her eyes on the last remaining fruit-filled pastry.

"There are no Fairy Circles anywhere near here." Aeron set his fork down and folded his arms on the tabletop. "We would know about them."

"It's outside the colony's territory. Past the open fields and in an oak tree forest. Fortyish miles to the north." Spurgle spoke fast, running his hands over a wooden scroll case hanging from a strap over his shoulder.

"You've been there?" Zanna turned, fixing Spurgle with a pointed glare.

"No."

"Then how do you know it's real? I'm sure someone would have documented it if there was a Fairy Circle within a hundred miles of here. They're rare."

"I have a map," said Spurgle, holding up the scroll case as if that were proof enough.

"You had two maps to this location?" Aeron tapped his claw-tipped nails on the table. One map was a fool's diversion, most likely a wild goose chase. There might be some validity with two…or an even wilder goose chase.

"Buying every map to a relic guarantees one less person I'm competing with to find it." Spurgle clutched the scroll case to his chest.

"Or someone keeps making copies, knowing someone will buy them," pointed out Zanna, rising to face Spurgle. She spread her wings, holding them stiff and high in warning.

"I win them at cards." Spurgle peered down his nose at her, but took a step back.

A wise move.

Princess was not pleased.

"My son is not a thief, and to prove it, we'll ask him. The kids go to the north often to pick wild grapes and plums along the creek," said Zanna, narrowing her eyes. "Aeron, why don't you come with us? You don't have anything important planned, do you?"

"Some meetings with—" started Aeron.

"You have nothing important planned," Zanna reiterated.

"My father would disagree." Aeron grabbed the rest of the liver on his plate and shoved it into his mouth. Breakfast appeared to be over, and he wasn't about to let that delicacy go to waste.

Zanna

"We set out immediately," Zanna said, glaring at Aeron's hand on her shoulder. He had let her go while he started his account of how their disastrous journey had begun. But he kept a hand on her, his curved nails digging into her leather spaulders.

"Sadly. I didn't get to ask for seconds." Aeron slumped, his lips curving down. "Did they have pâté for lunch? I'm starving."

"What is the point of pâté when you have teeth like yours?" Zanna set her eyes on his jaw. He smiled, showing off his massive, curved teeth.

"They're for shearing and biting, not grinding things into a paste that melts on the tongue."

Jude shuddered. "Probably serving it at a dinner. Maybe you should clean up first—"

"We're not done with the story."

It was a delay tactic to calm her down without the words being said. As much as she wanted to pull away and find Asher, Aeron was likely right in holding her back. In her current mood, there wouldn't be much left of the boy once she got done with him.

Ground him for life. Not allowed out of the castle for the next twenty years. Nobody would argue with me...well, Aeron would.

Aeron slid his hand into her hair—another soothing tactic. He was irritatingly good at that.

"His friends said he'd gone further up the creek. We went looking for him." Zanna's eyelids lowered.

Wild plum trees grew along the creek banks, shading the water with their overreaching branches. Berry bushes, sugarcane, wheat, and corn grew nearby in small fields irrigated by the creek. Fae children splashed in the stream, their laughter rising over the meadowlarks singing in the fields.

"I told you Asher has the map. He's following it," said Spurgle, gesturing down the creek with the scroll case. "Up the creek one mile, then it turns north."

"Asher knows better than to cross the border and leave the kingdom. He never has before." Zanna glided beside Spurgle, searching for any sign of Asher. There were only kids out enjoying a little time for fun before their summer chores and classes. "And he has geography today with my father. He wouldn't miss that for anything."

"He wouldn't miss it to go explore on his own? A Fairy Circle opens up an entirely new world for a curious young Fae. There might be a human house nearby. Your little social butterfly of a boy might go talk to them, and then what?" Spurgle rambled, his face turning red and a vein throbbing in his forehead.

"We blame you for leaving a map to a dangerous location out where a child found it," said Aeron. For a Naiad, he was remarkably slow to anger, but his tone carried a growl of warning that sent a delightful chill up her spine.

"I'm the victim!" Spurgle whined, his face paling.

She smirked, landing on a tree limb spanning the creek. The Naiads swimming nearby turned toward her and bowed their heads.

Zanna dropped her hands on her hip, her wings flared to frame her in orange and gold. "I'm looking for Prince Asher. Have you seen him?"

They chattered amongst themselves as Aeron and Spurgle alighted on the limb beside her.

"No, we haven't seen the prince this morning," said the biggest with a shrug. She held out a dark green hand. "Would you like us to look for him, Princess Zanna? We're supposed to be fishing today."

"Go on with what you're supposed to be doing." Zanna turned to Aeron and whispered, "Don't need to make Dad angry again by distracting anyone from their job."

"Yeah, the last time you did that...I thought he was going to ground you." Aeron kept his voice low.

"It's not like the royal guards do anything but stand around all day. I gave them a mission."

"You had them looking for a were coyote in the middle of a harvest festival. Panicked everyone."

"I know what I saw," huffed Zanna.

"What you saw was likely a Naiad in costume for Halloween. I'm willing to bet they were so embarrassed and afraid of you, that's why they never came forward," said Aeron, the corner of his lip rising in a fanged smirk.

"So disgusting. Stop wasting time flirting. You're married and we have more important things to do." Spurgle annoyingly reminded them of his presence.

"I still don't believe Asher took your map." Zanna stood on her toes and kissed Aeron.

Spurgle grumbled, unscrewing the end of the scroll case. He pulled out the map and narrowed his eyes. "Because he would have turned north before he reached the bend in the creek." His wings flared as he turned toward the scrubby trees rising in the distance. "He can't be too far ahead. Kid's given to distraction. I hear voices."

"I always wondered if you did." Zanna laughed, lifting her wings.

Spurgle gave her a dirty look. "There's kids playing in the trees."

"We'll ask them if they've seen Asher. If they haven't, we return to the castle and look for him there." Aeron's wings hummed as he hovered over the creek.

"He might even be there." Zanna passed her husband in a single flap of her broader wings.

Aeron

Aeron raked a hand through his hair. Dirt rained over his shoulders. It would take forever to get completely clean. Longer because he'd have to help Zanna.

"Asher had been in the oak trees with a few friends half an hour earlier," said Aeron.

"But nobody saw him with a map," added Zanna, narrowing her eyes. "But you know how convincing Spurgle can be when it's something important to him."

Aeron inhaled slowly and deeply, drawing a myriad of scents through his nose. Naiads, by nature, tracked prey with ease, above and below the water. Asher had stopped in one of the trees and taken to the air. The breeze had scattered his scent, making it impossible to tell which direction he had taken. The few Fae kids tending to half a dozen rabbits had no idea where he'd gone.

"This way," said Spurgle, dropping off a tree limb and gliding to the north as if he expected them to follow.

"You and I both know Asher didn't take that map," Zanna whispered, leaning toward him. "He would have made a copy in that book he carries everywhere."

"Yes, he would. Which worries me in other ways." Aeron scratched his chin, eyeing Spurgle vanishing through the trees. "Even if Spurgle is mistaken…Asher could still be wandering off on an adventure. Just because he's never crossed the border before doesn't mean he wouldn't now. He's almost thirteen. Naiads get a little more adventurous at that age."

"He's only half-Naiad," pointed out Zanna.

"With you as his mother." Aeron tilted his head and grinned.

Zanna pursed her lips, glaring at him from beneath her brows.

"I mean that as a compliment." He chuckled.

"You better." She rushed past, smacking his arm lightly. Her teeth flashed in a smile, a glimmer of mischief in her eyes.

Aeron flew after her, keeping his eyes open for any sign of Asher. There was none, and his scent faded.

A breeze raced through the massive oak branches. The forest ended abruptly in a rolling plain. Golden grass stretched as far as the eye could see. It shifted and swayed like water as the wind caressed it.

Spurgle led the way, dropping low. He skimmed the grass, one hand on the sword strapped to his hip. In the other, he gripped the scroll case. Zanna followed on one side, her eyes on the sky. Aeron flew on the other, watching the ground.

A sharp-eyed, red-tail hawk might see them as breakfast. Coyotes were the greatest danger in the grass, along with roadrunners. Scent marking deterred most predators. Destroying nests took care of the birds, but only to a point. They still wandered near the kingdom's boundaries in search of food.

Three strings of barbed wire cut across the plains. On the other side, a dozen longhorn cattle grazed. If they got out of the fence, they would wander into their fields and eat everything. Thankfully, the humans kept the fence in good shape. They were ideal neighbors, never wandering outside their boundaries. Even if they did, the veil that hid their cistern would disorient them, sending them back to where they came.

"I thought we'd see him by now," said Spurgle, landing on a gnarled wood post. He pulled out the map, flicking his wings. "The first marsh on the map isn't far."

"Yes, it doesn't move, but it should be dry this time of year." Zanna balanced on the barbed wire, her wings flared. "There are a lot of marshes and oak forests out there. How do you know it's the right one?"

"I can read a map." Spurgle rolled the parchment and jamming it into the scroll case.

Aeron hovered higher. He shaded his eyes, peering into the distance. Spurgle said their destination was fortyish miles away. If they pressed on at full speed, they would get there in a little over an hour. If Asher was indeed on this trail, he would not fly in the open.

"Asher wouldn't go this far alone. He would have friends with him, and all I smell are cows...and cow pies," said Aeron, landing beside Zanna. The steel was cool beneath his bare feet. "We didn't bring any food or water—"

"Is the mighty Aeron afraid of a little one-hour journey?" Spurgle looked over his shoulder, a leer twisting the corners of his mouth.

"You know that doesn't work on me. We should return home and look for Asher there." Aeron glanced back at where they had come from.

"If I didn't know better, I'd think you want us to fly all the way out there because nobody else would go with you." Zanna folded her arms and smirked at Spurgle.

Spurgle's expression slid like mud into a scowl.

"Lead the way," said Zanna, rolling her eyes. "But only because I want to see what kind of trouble you fall into on the way."

"This isn't necessary." Aeron tapped his clawed fingertips together, searching for the right words to get them home.

"No, but it'll be fun." She rose into the air, her brilliant golden-orange wings glowing in the sunlight.

"The kid *has* my map." Spurgle flew past Zanna, and they were off once again.

Zanna

Zanna glared at Jude. "I need to talk to Asher and make sure he doesn't have that map or try to follow it."

"I'll send for him. Would you like to clean up first? Go to the baths, and I'll have food brought down to you?" Jude offered, gesturing to one of the other guards.

"Send for Asher and prepare the baths. Nobody will want to be in there with us," said Aeron, stroking a hand down Zanna's arm. "Zanna, are you going to yell at Asher?"

"He *worried* me for hours!" Zanna shot back, her anger flaring once again. Heat surged through her body. Her fingers curled into her palms. "And there's still the matter of a missing map."

"He's not a thief."

"I know he's not a thief!"

"Then you shouldn't be mad at him. Kids are naturally worrisome. That's nothing new."

"I am going to be so disappointed if he stole that map," she admitted, her mood plummeting from fire to long-cold ashes. "That's why I'm mad! That's not like him at all."

"I'm sure the map was misplaced or Spurgle is mistaken." Aeron wrapped an arm around her shoulders, drawing her close.

"Where's Spurgle?" asked Jude, peering over their heads and into the opening.

"Keeping his distance if he knows what's good for him," Aeron growled, baring his fangs.

"We flew over several dry marshes and oak forests and saw nothing." Zanna leaned against him, continuing the story.

∞

Dead oak trees reached skeletal limbs to the clear blue sky. More limbs, bleached white by the sun, littered the ground. Dread crawled through Zanna's chest, the need to be vigilant rising. It might be hot and dry during the summers, but it had been decades since she'd seen so many dead trees.

"We should turn back," said Aeron, his eyes reflecting the sky. "There's nothing out here."

"I don't understand," grumbled Spurgle, turning the map around. He flew higher up the tree they had stopped in to rest. The parchment rustled as he held it at arm's length, squinting at it. "It should be here."

"Big surprise. There's no Fairy Circle." Zanna ran her tongue around her dry mouth. "There was a small spring in the last oak forest. We'll go back there and rest before going home."

"I think I have it—" started Spurgle, flicking his wings.

"No, we're going home." A growl rose from Aeron. He exploded into the air, his wings rasping sharply against each other. "Let me see that map."

"It's my map!" protested Spurgle, running down the limb.

"It's worthless. Hand it over." Aeron smacked into Spurgle, knocking him off the limb. They only fought for a second. The map ripped, half-caught in Aeron's clawed hand.

"You tore it!" Spurgle's wings caught him before he hit a branch...or the ground. His face flushed crimson as he flew back to Aeron.

"Stop fighting," snapped Zanna, flaring her wings. "We've had our fun, and it's time to go home. Asher didn't take your map. If he did, we'd have seen him along the way, and there's no sign or scent of him. Aeron?"

"He hasn't been here. Nobody has," replied Aeron, studying the piece of the map in his hands. His face contorted as he landed in front of Zanna. He thrust the scrap into her face, his wings upraised and stiff. "Take a look."

Zanna grumbled, taking the parchment. As far as she was concerned, this entire trip was only an excuse to stretch their wings. If there had been a Fairy Circle so close to home, they would have found it decades ago. She would know...and likely have gone through it at some point. Who wouldn't want to walk around as a human for a little while?

"What's wrong with this?" She squinted at the map. Something was off, but what? Slowly, she turned it, comparing it to the rest of the map in Spurgle's hands. "Bring me the rest of the map. Which side is up?"

"The compass is backward and upside down," huffed Aeron.

"Of course it is. You don't think a map to a Fairy Circle would be straightforward, do you?" Spurgle joined them, turning his part of the map for Zanna to see. "You must have a keen eye to work through these kinds of tricks."

"Where's the Fairy Circle? We followed the map you were reading, and there's nothing here. You couldn't read a regular map, let alone any kind of encoded map. We're going home now." Aeron took the air again, circling warily with a hand on his sword hilt. "Zanna?"

She nodded, throwing the parchment at Spurgle.

He dove after it, swearing.

Aeron

"Well, that was pointless," Jude said, looking from one to the other. "But it doesn't explain how you ended up like...this." He gestured to their dirt-encrusted bodies.

"We wanted to get home fast, but it was already hot, and we needed to rest." Aeron lowered his head, his wings dropping flat against his back. "It was a mistake."

"I didn't want you to shrivel up and blow away." Zanna smiled, patting his arm.

"And I appreciate that," he said, chuckling. "But we should have come home..."

∞

Cooling mud oozed between Aeron's webbed toes. Massive oak branches shaded a section of a tiny creek. The water trickled into a few pools. A few minnows splashed in the shallows, attempting to work their way down with the flow of water.

He licked his lips, pondering a quick snack. Neither Zanna nor Spurgle would join him for a meal of raw fish. They would insist on cooking it, which would take time. His stomach rumbled, but wasting so much meat he couldn't carry it back to the colony was against their laws.

"Fold here and here. Tuck here." Zanna stood on a knotted root overhanging the pool. In her hands was a piece of leaf she had cut with one of her throwing knives. She twisted and folded it with growing frustration. "Why is this always so hard?"

Spurgle landed higher in the tree. He dropped into a crook and sat with his arms folded. "This map was a decoy, but the other map is real. I bet your son's at the Fairy Circle right now."

"Shut up about my son!" shouted Zanna.

A gleaming blade thudded into the wood near Spurgle's head. He jerked around, his eyes widening as he stared at it.

"Asher's debt is paid. He's been cleaning up after you for two months now, and your leg looks fine." Zanna dropped the leaf, another dagger in hand. She waved it in Spurgle's general direction, daring him to say another word. "I swear if you so much as look at Asher with any kind of accusation, I'll carve an I into your face so everyone knows what an idiot you are."

Spurgle's face went from red to white in a flash.

"Zanna, as much as I'd like to see you do that, you can't do that," Aeron said, kneeling to gather water in his hands. He peered into the darkness beneath the tree's exposed roots. Nothing dangerous there. "No matter how much he deserves it."

"I'm not the one who stole my map," mumbled Spurgle, rolling so that he was entirely out of sight on the branch. "Couldn't we find a better place to rest? Smells like skunk."

"I'm going to—" Zanna started with a hiss. She froze, her gaze going over Aeron's head.

A shadow fell across the creek. Aeron leaped sideways, splashing through the knee-high water. Slender paws fell where he had been. A long, narrow muzzle, greyish-brown and filled with teeth, appeared overhead. Zanna dropped into the water, her sword drawn and flashing. Another set of paws danced around her. White teeth snapped at her head.

Coyotes.

Aeron flew into Zanna, pushing her beneath the water. If they tried to fly, the coyotes would certainly catch one of them. The water was too shallow to escape that way. He carried her beneath the old tree's submerged roots.

Zanna sputtered, clinging to his chest plate. There was a small cavity in the trunk where the water had washed away the earth. Whines came from outside as the coyotes dug at the bark. A suffocating stench filled Aeron's nose.

"Are you okay?" She brushed her hair out of her eyes.

"Didn't touch me." Aeron narrowed his eyes. Rotten wood and mud surrounded them. The water stirred as a paw slid beneath them. "I'm going to push you up. See if you can find an opening or something."

"It reeks in here," muttered Zanna, turning in his arms. He grasped her around her hips and lifted her slowly. Her wings hung heavy over her back, coated in muck. "Nothing but mud. Can't get a handhold."

Aeron lifted her higher.

"There's roots up further," she said, sliding out of his hands.

He followed, crawling through thick mud. Embedded rocks scraped his hands and feet. The suffocatingly thick air carried a hint of blood... Zanna's blood.

Nails scraped on the bark. The coyotes' whines mixed with a hiss.

"Move slowly," whispered Zanna, pulling him onto firm ground. Dirt rained down upon them. The coyotes had moved from the creek to the bank.

Aeron swallowed as hazy light pierced the darkness. His nictating membrane slid over his eyes, protecting them from dust. They weren't alone. An agitated skunk swished its black and white tail before them. It stamped its feet, hissing louder. Their shrill, excited yapping bounced off the inside of the den. They continued digging, opening a wide hole in the base of the tree above.

Having had more than enough, the skunk spun. Noxious fumes filled the confined space. There was no escape, but the coyotes fled. Thankfully, they didn't appear desperate enough to push through the stench.

Zanna gagged, slapping her hands over her mouth and nose. Her eyes watered as Aeron grabbed her shoulders. The skunk stood facing them, baring its fangs. It stamped its feet and spun again, swinging its tail toward them.

They ran for the opening, but couldn't avoid a direct hit from the skunk. The stench followed them as they fled. It was everywhere, clinging to their clothes and in their mouths. Coughing and retching, Aeron flew directly up into the tree. Zanna followed, beating her wings to keep the fumes away from her nose. The spray had covered them and there was no escaping it until they shed their armor and scrubbed their skin raw.

The coyotes watched from a safe distance away. Their tongues lolled out of their mouths as they panted. The skunk didn't emerge, hissing from its den.

"Where's Spurgle?" Tears ran down Zanna's face as she squinted, looking at where he had been when the coyotes attacked.

"Coward probably fled the moment the coyotes appeared," said Aeron, rubbing his nose.

"I'm going to kill him." Zanna curled her fingers like claws and raked the air. "At least severely claw up his face. This is all his fault! We wasted all this time, and Asher might have his missing map or drawn one of his own! He could be lost! We have to get home and form a search party!"

Aeron set his jaw, fluttering his wings in a vain effort to get rid of the skunk odor. Jumping to conclusions was a skill Zanna had mastered when they were children. She'd need time to settle down, and under no circumstances would he tell her to calm down. It was best to let her run through whatever chain of logic she followed until it broke.

"No time to waste," he said, glancing at his wings. The worst of the mud had fallen off. "Can you fly?"

"Well enough," she replied, rising awkwardly into the air. She hovered, still-wet mud covering her wing scales. "Find Asher…then deal with Spurgle."

Aeron nodded, grimacing at the thought of what she would do to the idiot if she caught him in her current mood. It wouldn't be pretty.

Zanna

"We flew straight back home. No stops." Zanna stomped in place. More dirt fell onto the pile at her feet.

"We're relieved that Asher is safe," Aeron said, patting Zanna's shoulder. "Right, honey? No yelling at the boy?"

"Uhm, what's going on?" Asher appeared in the doorway with the guard that had been sent for him. The boy's green eyes grew large beneath his curly brown hair. He stepped back, pinching his nose. "I didn't do anything, I swear. I went to the creek this morning, then lessons, then out to the creek again, and had a blackberry fight. You'll find my stained clothes in the laundry. That's the worst thing I did!"

Zanna melted, rushing toward her son to grab him and hold him in her arms. He cried out, running from her.

"There's the troublemaker!" Spurgle's voice rang through the entry. He dropped onto the flight balcony, waving a hand over his face. "What is that stench? What-what happened to you two?"

"You..." Zanna whirled upon him, her wings at full flare. She stopped and looked over her shoulder at Asher. The boy stared back at her from behind Jude. "Asher, did you take Spurgle's map this morning while cleaning his study?"

"What? No, I rolled it up and put it away in his case. He showed me how he stored them. You can check the case he's carrying. That's the one I put it in. It's purple for Fairy Circle." Asher spoke quickly, pointing at the case that Spurgle had been carrying the entire time.

A guttural snarl rose from Aeron, the fin on his head popping upright. His wings rattled, and he started toward Spurgle.

"Wh-what?" Spurgle sputtered, clutching the scroll case tube in both hands. "I left it on my desk..."

"You done screwed up something awful, Spurgle," whispered Jude, dropping a hand on Asher's shoulder.

Zanna drew her sword, waving the tip toward Spurgle. "Aeron, dear, is this serious enough for an I on the cheek or straight down the middle of his face?"

"Cheek is sufficient. I'll hold him," said Aeron viciously. "Then I'll shred his wings."

"I left the map on my desk," Spurgle whined, backpedaling to the balcony's edge.

"You have until I count to ten," said Zanna, glancing at Aeron. "To make it fair."

"Twenty," added Aeron. "To make it fun."

"One."

"Two."

"Why aren't you flying?"

Spurgle whined, his entire body shaking. Without another word, he spun and leaped into the air. He wobbled, almost running into several Fae who had stopped to watch the exchange.

Zanna's wings twitched, held high and stiff as if preparing to fly. They'd wasted more time on Spurgle than he deserved. Her wings fell. She sheathed her sword and turned with a smile to Asher. Aeron turned with her, laughing.

"You two are so weird," said Asher, still hiding behind Jude.

"Why don't you come over here and give us a hug." Zanna spread her arms.

Asher's face wrinkled around his nose.

"No reason to punish the boy." Aeron swept Zanna into his arms. "Down to the bath for us. I'm sure we'll have it all to ourselves!"

"Send someone with whatever we have to get rid of this smell!" Zanna shouted as Aeron carried her through the doorway and into the hall. The remaining guards pressed themselves to the walls as they passed.

"So that map doesn't go anywhere?" Asher called after them.

"It's a fake," said Aeron, turning back toward Asher.

"Good to know." Asher smiled far too broadly, his hand resting on the bulging leather bag that hung off his hip.

"Told you so," whispered Zanna.

Aeron shook his head, grumbling under his breath. "Kid's too smart for his own good."

"Just like his mother." She looped her arms around Aeron's neck and pressed her lips to his. They recoiled from each other, sticking their tongues out.

"I still taste the skunk! It's all over you!" Aeron exclaimed, continuing down the hallway.

Zanna gagged. "I'm going to throw up."

"Not on me!"

They broke into laughter as Fae fled from their approach.

The Colorado Incident

Sherri Mines

Legend says if you make an offering to the Monkey God, he will grant your every desire. It is also said he will use that desire to bring about the end of the world. No one knows the truth. And if you're lucky, you will never find out

CLASSIFIED MEMORANDUM RE: COLORADO INCIDENT
TO: Federal Bureau of Investigation, Attn: [REDACTED], Washington D.C.
From: Ronald J. Allen, ASAC-SI, Denver FBI Field Office
Information regarding the disappearance of Silver Station, Colorado.
INTERVIEW (EXCERPTED): Oren Clay (O.C.) Edwards, survivor.
Note: Excerpt from multiple interviews with Mr. Edwards. A crusty gentleman in his late fifties, he is quick to anger when his word is questioned, necessitating multiple breaks and a change in interviewers. Mr. Edwards is employed by Sandia Labs as their troubleshooter. I spoke with Mr. Edwards's manager, [REDACTED], and was told, "If he says it's true, it's true."

Agent One: [REDACTED], original interviewer.

Agent Two: [REDACTED], replacement interviewer.

BEGIN INTERVIEW

Agent 1: Were you there when Silver Station went missing?

Edwards: Yes, I was there when the town went missing. I'll tell you the story, but you won't believe me. Some of it was pretty surreal.

Agent 1: Why were you in the area? Tell us in your own words what happened.

Edwards: I was between projects, and had some time to sightsee before moving on to Denver. Did the usual tourist stuff: the Million Dollar Highway, Mesa Verde, museums, and mine tours. I even rented a cabin and soaked in the hot springs near Pagosa. That was nice.

The trouble started the morning I left Pagosa. Blue skies, fluffy white clouds, and the air smelled fresh and clean. Turned onto Hwy 160, headed down the mountain, and enjoyed the scenery. Half an hour into the drive, light gray clouds drifted in with a light rain. Conditions continued to deteriorate, and dark clouds and heavy rain had set in.

That final descent down the mountain was eerie. The narrow road was steep with multiple curves, forcing me to drive at a slow pace. Small clumps of homes and businesses clung to the hillside with no signs of life, the buildings dark and looking abandoned. The lights of a small town beckoned in the valley below, encouraging me onward, if I could just get off this damn road.

A thick fog had settled in the valley by the time I passed the sign welcoming me to Silver Station. A normal two-hour drive had taken me over five hours. I was cold, and discouraged, and not a happy camper. Out of nowhere, the Grand Silver Hotel sign appeared like a beacon in the fog, and lit the corner of the old stone building with a cheerful glow. Maybe this bad day was about to get better. My vacation was coming to an end, and I had no desire to spend the rest of the day driving slowly in crappy weather. To hell with it—I was stopping early for the night.

Stepping into the lobby confirmed my decision. The historic building felt authentic. Bright Victorian wallpaper and antique-looking stuffed chairs complemented the crystal wall lamps and the polished wood of the front reception desk.

"Welcome to the Grand Silver Hotel, established in 1886. Do you have a reservation, sir?"

"No reservation. Do you have a room for tonight?"

"Let me check, we are almost full." The clerk consulted his list. "I do have one of the original inside rooms available. It's one of our smaller rooms, and has no windows."

"I thought windows were required in hotel rooms?"

"I assure you, sir, the room is legal. There are exceptions for older buildings. A copy of the regulations is available, if you would like to review them. Would you like the room?"

I agreed, checked in quickly, and signed the hotel register. The clerk handed me an old-fashioned key. The style matched the hotel, with a large brass tag embossed with my room number and the name of the hotel. It was different, but I liked it. A polished wooden staircase at the end of the lobby led me upstairs to my room. Small, but nicely furnished with antiques and the bed looked inviting. A nap after lunch sounded appealing.

A table covered in plates caught my eye while being seated: cheeseburger, fries, a milkshake, and a pile of empties. When I looked at the table again, a thin, dark-haired man with gray at the temples was determinedly eating his way through a piece of pie à la mode. His blue denim shirt hung on his thin body, and he gave the impression of being down on his luck. My thought was he had to miss a few meals, and was now making up for lost days.

A battered blue backpack on the chair next to him rustled, and a head began to slowly rise out of the top. The man firmly pushed the head down and zipped up the backpack. My impression was he was hiding a pet. The server stepped in front of my table, blocking my view for a moment while she put down my lunch and refilled my coffee. The table was empty when she moved away.

The gift shop was a pleasant surprise, with a nice selection of local history books next to the usual souvenirs and snacks. The friendly clerk rang up my purchase of couple of local mining books, and a science fiction novel from a local author, Sarah somebody. The bed was very comfortable; I took a short nap, and read for a couple of hours. The novel was pretty good, about a lost history, and energy pods that grew on trees.

On my way to dinner, I stuck my head in the saloon for a minute. A restored wooden back bar with mirror, red flocked wallpaper, and a large portrait of a buxom woman dressed in white gauze gave the saloon an old Western throwback vibe that was perfect for a drink or two. I was looking forward to stopping by later that evening.

The restaurant was very busy. I added my name to the sign-up sheet, and sat in the waiting area. While I was waiting, a couple stood nearby, and talked about a guy they saw that morning. He was sitting on the ground by a large group of rocks, feeding leafy branches and some kind of thick, dark reddish liquid into a charcoal grill. The grill produced a dark and greasy smoke that smelled terrible. When my name was called, they were still arguing: one wanted to call the police, and the other wanted to ignore it.

The server led me to my table, and warned me of a delay before taking my order. I was studying the menu when an electric tingle went down my arms. Everyone was frozen. Diners had forks halfway to their mouths, and a server was in midstride carrying a tray of food.

That's when a man and woman in costume appeared, dripping wet from the storm.

I remember being confused. There was no Renaissance Faire nearby. The red-haired woman wore a Celtic-style outfit of a black skirt, and a long cloak of green and black tartan. She carried a small harp. The man was tall and reminded me of a blonde Viking, with a knee-length embroidered tunic, a wide leather belt, and beads in his beard. A bone whistle hung around his neck. At his feet, a large rodent—yes, I said rodent—as tall as the man's knee watched the room. The two strangers came over and sat at my table.

Agent One: Do you expect me to believe this tale, Mr. Edwards? People in costume? Large rodent? How much did you have to drink before dinner?

Edwards: I was not drinking! I'm telling you the truth. Someone should know what really happened, so I agreed to talk to you. If you don't like it, we can end this interview right now!

[The interview was stopped until the next day. Agent One was replaced by Agent Two. The interview continued.]

Agent Two: Our apologies, Mr. Edwards. Please continue with your recollection.

Edwards: Thank you. As I said, I was not drinking. But I wish I'd visited the saloon and had a drink there before it disappeared.

The woman gestured. "Say nothing about us—we are invisible to others. A terrible storm is coming tonight, to conceal the first battle of the gods. You must go upstairs to your room and stay there. The lack of windows will make it difficult for the creature to get to you."

The Viking spoke up. "The Monkey God has been seen. Spurgle has been making offerings nearby." His deep voice was solemn.

"Monkey God? Spurgle? Gods aren't real. I'm not buying whatever you are selling. Go away, and bother someone else."

She laughed, a tinkling sound, and held out her hand. A blue flame danced on her palm. "Of course the gods are real. These days, they choose to hide in plain sight. You can call me...Eadon." She closed her hand and gestured at the Viking. "Call him...Humli."

Normally, I would have told them to leave, but this was not a normal situation. Everyone was frozen. The floor was dry where they walked. A large rodent traveled with them. They knew about my room. She held a flame in her hand. Okay, then. "Well, what can you tell me? How long will I be upstairs?"

Eadon held out her hand. "For this night only. Give me your key." Humli placed his hand on top of hers. A blue glow surrounded their hands, then faded. She put the key in my palm, and closed my fingers over it. "Keep this key with you at all times. It will help to protect you, and will prevent the creature from entering your room."

She patted my hand. "Get your dinner and go upstairs quickly. Lock your door and stay in your room. Do not call attention to yourself. We can contain the battle for tonight. Come down tomorrow after the storm passes and we will explain as much as we can."

The rodent tugged on the Viking's tunic, and whispered in his ear as he leaned over. "We have to go. Spurgle is making another offering."

"Again? What the hell is wrong with this man? Doesn't he realize..." Their voices faded as they disappeared. The tingle went away, and people started to move again. I gave up my table and bought a sandwich and water from the grab-and-go kiosk by the door, went upstairs and locked the deadbolt behind me.

Agent Two: Why did you decide to follow their orders?

Edwards: I just told you. Everyone frozen, the flame in her hand... My brain decided they were telling the truth, and I should go along with it. Plus, their sense of urgency was so strong, you could almost touch it.

I jotted a few notes about my interesting day in my notebook, before turning on the TV and eating my dinner. The local meteorologists were puzzled by the sudden storms and peculiar weather formations in this part of Colorado, and admitted they had no idea what was happening. After the weather, there was an "odd news" segment: the police were receiving multiple reports of stuffed monkeys peering into people's windows. The amused announcers attributed the story to too much summer partying.

About forty-five minutes after the weather report, the room went dark. My pocket flashlight came in handy: I washed up quickly and laid down fully dressed on top of the bed. Turned off the flashlight, held my room key, and listened.

My room was in the middle of the hotel with no windows, and should have been nice and quiet. That night, the experience was like sleeping in a corner room, complete with movement and sound. The building creaked and shuddered, buffeted by the storm. I could hear heavy rain. The sound of the wind rose and fell, alternating between groans, howls, and grumbles as it whipped down the hallway.

Around midnight, there was a sense of someone or something outside my door that felt dark, and wrong. It hissed, and I knew it wanted in. Time to stay still: I breathed through my nose, tried to blank my thoughts, and clutched the room key tighter. It seemed an eternity before the presence moved away from the door and faded. The storm continued for hours. Too wired to sleep, I eventually drifted off despite the noise, still holding the key.

I awoke from a strange dream when the lights came on. Tried the local weather, but a "No Signal" message floated across the TV screen on every channel. No signal on my phone, either. Coffee, yes. Coffee would be good. Downstairs, the clerk at the reception desk looked up.

"This building was damaged in last night's storm. Everyone must check out and evacuate the town immediately."

He spoke in an odd, monotonous voice. Something tried to compel me to agree and leave. Without thinking, the room key was in my hand. The clerk looked away, and the compulsion faded.

Fresh air sounded good. I stepped out the front door to clear my head and to check the weather. The air had a weird blue tinge, like peering through a window of colored glass. Fast-moving clouds made feathery patterns in the sky, and the air was heavy with moisture. People acted odd: they walked in a mechanical, almost robotic manner, or were driving with vacant-looking faces.

I really needed some coffee to process all...this. I went inside, and found an empty restaurant. A steady drip, drip, drip of water from the ceiling splashed into a yellow bucket. The ceiling drip and a couple of cracked windows seemed to be the only damage. Someone coughed behind me. The costumed people (and the rodent) were back. Eadon and Humli walked into the restaurant. The rodent stayed at the door, watching the lobby.

She gestured at the kitchen. "We need you to gather supplies for ten days and head towards the mountains. You will be guided to a safe shelter. Do not leave the shelter until you can see the entire valley in sunlight and the storms have cleared. Only then may you come down and rejoin your world."

Humli reached inside his bag, and produced an embossed leather-bound journal. On top of the journal was a beautifully crafted wooden pen with a golden lightning bolt on the cap. "Take this, and write down everything you see and feel. You have been chosen to bear witness, and to create a record of what will occur."

I laughed. "I deal in logic, not feelings. You have the wrong guy."

He took my hand and placed it on top of the journal. I felt a light electrical buzz. "You have hidden talents we need. You *must* do this."

Eadon continued, "Fill your vehicle with gas as you leave town. An animal friend will join you there and stay with you on the mountain. Do NOT pick up anyone or take anything you are offered. We are holding the peril at bay for now. Gather your things and go quickly. Keep your windows up no matter what happens during your drive. If the doors are locked and the windows are up, it cannot get in."

"What are you afraid of?"

They glanced at each other, then at me. "The Monkey God takes many forms. It has been released from its prison, and is expressing its...displeasure."

Humli muttered something under his breath about "Idiot Spurgle."

"Should I bring food for more than ten days? Just in case."

"No. If we cannot defeat the Monkey God in ten days, the world will be destroyed. Many gods are moving in to contain the problem." She threw her arm out and pointed. "Now go!"

Agent Two: What were the names of the gods they mentioned?

Edwards: I don't know. The only names I heard were Eadon and Humli.

Agent Two: Do you have a detailed list of the items you took from the hotel?

Edwards: No, I do not have a detailed list. I want you to understand that I. Do. Not. Steal. But considering the situation, following their instructions seemed the safest thing to do.

First, I went looking for coffee. It was cold, but I drank two large cups, anyway. Next, I boxed up perishables and cans of non-perishables from the kitchen, and took a couple of sandwiches from the grab-and-go kiosk. I also took some cases of water, over-the-counter medicines from the gift shop, more history books, and another novel from that Sarah woman. Packed my SUV, rolled up my windows, and turned my vehicle towards the tall "Gas" sign in the distance.

The Gas-N-Shop was on the far edge of town. No cars, no people. I used my credit card at the pump to fill up with gas, and went inside to scavenge. Picked up a first-aid kit, toilet paper, and some food. Okay, a lot of food. The giant cans from the restaurant were just not practical for one person. I left them behind, in case someone else could use them, and stocked up with individual meals, protein bars, jerky, and snacks. And some frozen mac-n-cheese. And a few cupcakes.

The last load was in my hands when I spied an oversized gray cat with lynx-like ears sitting regally in the front seat. She was about the size of a bobcat with long fur and huge white paws. Best guess is she was a Maine Coon or a Norwegian Forest Cat.

"Hello. Since you got in a locked car, you must be the animal friend joining me. Excuse me while I acquire a few last-minute items inside." I looked her up and down. "You're a big cat. I hope they have enough food for you." She blinked her light-green eyes, looking bored. Litter and cat food was added to the supplies in back. As we pulled out of the gas station, a golden glow on the hills below Mount Pintada gave us our destination.

You know, [REDACTED], I've built a career on logic. But that day, I drove up to the mountains with a large cat to hide for ten days, based upon the word of two people I did not know, who were dressed in costumes. [*Mr. Edwards shook his head*] I still can't believe I did that.

I tried to talk to the cat as we crossed the valley, but she ignored me. At one point during the drive, I looked over and said, "You have a hell of a lot of hair. I think I'm going to call you Fluffy." She made a chuffing sound and turned away. That's when I knew she understood me.

We were passing a large group of rocks when a man ran out in to the middle of the road waving his arms. I slammed on the brakes, and barely missed him. It was the man from the restaurant! He was disheveled, and had somehow acquired a white streak in his hair. A stuffed monkey was in his backpack, and peered over his shoulder with a wide grin. The man spoke frantically, his sentences running together into one long string as he knocked on the window and pulled on the door. "Open the window and talk to me! Please, for the love of God take me with you I need to get out of this place. Please! I didn't mean to do it! I had no idea this would happen! I just wanted to be rich! Let me in!"

Fluffy stood up. Her back raised, her fur puffed straight out, and she growled at the man (and monkey) with a deep, guttural sound. I put my foot on the accelerator and gently moved forward, almost hitting him as I drove away. He was still pleading. "If you won't open the door, take the backpack. Please!"

When I looked in the rearview mirror, I swear the stuffed monkey turned its head and talked to the man. Fluffy sat back down and stared out the windshield.

"I guess that was Spurgle." She didn't answer.

We turned at the stop sign and headed for Mount Pintada. Clouds swirled along the tops of the mountains, as if the storm was prevented from entering the valley. The weird blue tinge was back, giving the scenery a distorted look. We were alone on the road. I heard a female voice in my head whisper, *We need to hurry; they can't hold it much longer.* I looked over at Fluffy, but she was staring out the window.

The curves got tighter, and the road narrowed to a single lane. We kept climbing as the rain came down in torrents. The windshield wipers could not keep up, and forced me to slow to a crawl in order to see. Fluffy was very still, her eyes tightly closed like she was concentrating.

CRACK! A bolt of lightning struck the road ahead, briefly illuminating a pair of wrought iron gates that opened as we arrived. We drove through the gates, went down a curved driveway, and into a stone-clad garage with the door up. I parked, got out and flipped the light switch. An antique lightbulb lit the corner of the garage, the stairs leading up to the house, and a refrigerator next to the stairs. It was quick work to load the refrigerator and freezer sections with food and a case of water. A few bottles would go in the freezer later after they chilled to substitute for ice blocks in case the power went off.

I decided to brave the rain and walked over to a large grassy ledge overlooking the valley. There was nothing visible around me but a rock face and the ledge. I remember thinking the house must be on the other side. Purple and white lightning flashed nearby, encouraging me to stop looking and take shelter. I hustled back to the garage, moved our remaining items next to the stairs, then closed and locked up the garage before heading up the stairs and into the house for the first time.

I stopped dead. Our shelter was chiseled into the rock walls, creating a snug cave. A large glass wall sealed the opening, with a view of the ledge and the valley below. At the far end was Silver Station. The rest of the valley was a patchwork of green fields, farms, homes and buildings. I was stunned, and confused: there was no glass wall when I walked out on the ledge a few minutes ago. I still don't know how that trick was pulled off.

Agent Two: Tell me more about your shelter.

Edwards: The clear glass wall provided plenty of light for the living room and the mini kitchen behind it. A large comfortable-looking couch with tables at each end faced the window. The narrow bookcase in the corner held an inviting collection of books and knickknacks, waiting to be explored. Next to the kitchen, a door revealed a hallway with more surprises: I found a couple of bedroom suites, a laundry nook, and a cat room.

Fluffy and I were hungry, so we sat on the couch and ate sandwiches. Well, I ate the sandwiches and she ate most of the meat from the center. She was a bit friendlier once we shared a meal, and supervised as I put away our supplies, chose the first bedroom and unpacked. A battery-powered lantern in the bedrooms was the only source of illumination. Fluffy pointed out the flap at the bottom of the hallway door, to be lowered at night to block any light. The voice in my head whispered, *No visible lights at night; you need to stay hidden.*

When I returned to the living room, a massive cloud of orange dust was rolling into the valley, and a pair of binoculars had appeared on the side table. I picked them up and moved to the window. There was...something in front of the dust storm. Using the binoculars, I could see four riders in front of the storm wearing dark clothing and cowboy hats, their faces obscured. Each rider was on a different colored horse: black, white, chestnut, and I swear the last horse looked bluish with a black head. Their hooves gave off sparks as they danced in front of the storm. The sight took my breath away, and a song about ghost riders played in my head as I watched them cross the valley.

As the dust storm reached the edge of Silver Station, white clouds floated in and obscured our view. All we could see was an orange tinge lighting the clouds from below.

That first day, we kept checking the window. I looked out periodically and started my journal. Fluffy napped. When I wrote, there was a faint electrical buzz in my fingertips, and the golden lightning bolt in the pen cap glowed. All day, the orange-tinged clouds stayed with us. Our dinner was a carton of the restaurant's soup, plus a package of rolls, eaten cold.

[*Edwards laughed*] Fluffy refused to eat the cat food, and insisted on eating whatever I was having. After dinner, I learned about the magic running our snug little cave.

Agent Two: Did you say magic cave, Mr. Edwards?

Edwards: Yes, you heard me, I said magic. No other explanation fits. For example, the refrigerator in the garage worked without electricity. There was no cord, no outlet on the wall to plug it into.

Fluffy showed me the magic box in the kitchen, covered in carved symbols from multiple cultures: petroglyphs, runes, and others I did not recognize. One symbol on top was inlaid with gold, a different symbol inlaid with silver. I thought it was a fancy wooden storage box, and said out loud, "How am I supposed to cook and clean without a stove or a sink?" Fluffy jumped up on the counter and headbutted the door. I pulled the door down, she batted my dirty spoon into the box, then hit the side of the bowl. I took the hint, put the dirty bowl inside, and closed the door. She touched the silver symbol with her paw: all the carvings on the box glowed silver for about a minute, then faded. I opened the door and pulled out a clean bowl and spoon. Huh. Through trial and error, I learned touching the gold symbol would boil water or cook our meal. It made our lives a lot easier.

Agent Two: So the magic box cooked food and cleaned the dishes?

Edwards: You think I made up the whole magic bit. It's true. I can personally attest that I saw the magic box broil a steak to medium rare, bake a large potato, then cook a batch of green beans to perfection. I have no idea how it worked, but it's a bachelor's dream. I wish I had one.

The washing machine was another magic box. Add your dirty clothes, push the button, and pull out clean, dry clothes in an hour.

Agent Two: How did the bathroom magic work?

Edwards: That's kind of a private matter. [*Sigh*] Let's just say the bathroom was quirky, but got the job done.

Agent Two: What did you do all day?

Edwards: Fluffy and I shared a trait: extremely grumpy when we woke up. First thing every morning was a batch of cowboy coffee. Not my favorite, but it did the job. Two mugs of black coffee for me, and the remainder for Fluffy. She preferred hers in a bowl with a splash of milk and a half packet of sugar.

We quickly established a routine after coffee. I watched the weather, made notations in the journal, then read one of the books from the gift shop or the bookcase. Fluffy alternated between staring outside, patrolling the rooms, and taking naps.

The weather on our ledge and over the valley was both fascinating and terrifying. We saw heavy wind gusts, hailstones the size of golf balls, and multi-colored lightning storms above the clouds. It changed constantly, and was rarely the same twice. One afternoon, the clouds changed direction so quickly it reminded me of a flock of birds, or a school of sardines. We watched those clouds moving for hours. The following day, a black cloud moved us from right to left, a waterfall of dark gray rain cascading from the bottom of the cloud.

Items would randomly blow past our window: bushes, trees, a billboard saying "Visit Silver Station," they all went by. One day we saw a cow, a farm truck, and a white picket fence. I told Fluffy if I saw an older woman on a bicycle go by the window wearing a long-sleeve, button-down prairie dress, I was going to lock myself in the bedroom and stay there.

Once or twice a day, we would get a glimpse of the valley floor. The view was alway blurry, even with the binoculars. Most of the time, glowing blue balls of something flew through the air, randomly hitting the ground or a dome that glowed yellow on impact. Or vice versa, yellow balls hitting a blue dome. It was too blurry to make out details.

I wrote constantly. It became an obsession to document everything I saw and experienced. Sometimes it felt like my hand was possessed by another, and it tried to move faster than I could write. The journal was as magical as our cave: no matter how much I wrote, there was always another blank page, and the pen never ran out of ink.

At night we followed a routine to keep the front of the house dark: close the hallway door, lower the flap, and close the bedroom door before turning on the lantern. Fluffy slept at the foot of my bed. Twice she managed to sneak out before I got up, and was on the couch, waiting for me to make her coffee. No idea how she managed to get past the closed bedroom and hallway doors.

[*Mr. Edwards asked for a minute to compose himself, closing his eyes and taking deep breaths*]

BOOM! We woke to loud thunder that shook the bed. Fluffy jumped off and disappeared. I found her staring out at a storm right up against our window. The winds swirled. Large fist-sized hail pummeled the glass. The thunder continued to boom, and a sickly yellow glow appeared in the distance. It drifted closer, and coalesced into a man-like shape with a semblance of the stuffed monkey head from Spurgle's backpack. A vague smell of rotting meat wafted through the cave. The monkey opened its mouth, revealing large pointed fangs, and snarled. Its voice repeated over and over:

"Mine. Mine to destroy. Mine."

My heart was pounding, my chest tight. It was hard to breathe. My knees buckled, and I sat down hard on the couch, afraid. Fluffy grew larger, reaching the size of a lion. She stood on her hind legs, put her front paws on the glass, hissed and snarled at the creature outside the window. A movement to the left caught my eye. It was the pen, lit by a faint blue aura. The lightning bolt on the cap had changed to a deep red, and pulsed slowly. *Throw it.* Confused, I stayed seated. Cutting through the noise, a voice said very clearly, *Throw. The. Pen.* Slowly moving, trying not to attract the monkey's attention, I picked up the pen, aimed just to the left of Fluffy, and threw it as hard as I could.

The pen stuck to the window with a bright blue flare, the lightning bolt a blazing red. The creature yelped, and backed away as the thunder grumbled, then quieted. Fluffy kept making that low guttural sound. The storm slowly retreated from our ledge. Gray clouds returned to obscure our view. The fear was gone.

Fluffy returned to her normal size. She jumped up on the couch and laid a paw on my leg. "Thank you, Fluffy." I reached over to scratch her ears, but she pushed my hand aside, gave it one lick, then walked over to the other end of the couch, still watching the window. She remained on guard duty all morning, not eating or drinking. At some point, the pen returned to its normal place on top of the journal.

Much later, I realized this was the only time I heard or smelled anything from outside while we were in our cave. This happened on day five.

I was resting my eyes after lunch when a clattering noise woke me up. Fluffy chased a brush around on the floor, batting it over to me. She must have found it in the cat room. She jumped up on the couch, and sat in a regal pose, her nose in the air. I brushed her carefully from her head to her tail. [*Laughter*] I had to clean the brush four times! After being brushed to her satisfaction, Fluffy knocked the brush off the couch and batted it away. I think she was trying to lighten the mood.

That evening, the clouds rolled back, revealing an angry, deep red sky gradually fading into a sickly yellow. Balls of fire and sparks of red and yellow shot upwards, and disappeared. Years ago, I was in Hawaii and witnessed the Kilauea eruption at night. This display had the same look and feel, as though the volcano was below us in the valley.

On our sixth morning, we woke up to gray clouds hovering over the valley floor, lit from below with flashes of red, blue, and yellow lights. They dissolved a few hours later. A battle raged below us. Multiple figures were in a loose circle around a tall ape-like creature. The binoculars helped, but I had trouble making out the details. The perspective would shift, moving in and out, closer, then far away. My hand started writing in the journal involuntarily, and I became a conduit for whoever was recording the battle.

Agent Two: Tell me more about the battle.

Edwards: I can only remember fragments: someone in dark clothing with a hood fighting with a staff, a woman in a chariot shooting arrows, and a white buffalo charging the creature while a large wolf darted in and out as it snapped at the creature's heels. A man with multiple arms threw a lasso over the creature. A tall regal woman threw balls of a glowing red substance at its head. A man in light-colored clothing on horseback circled the creature, shooting a rifle. I saw a figure with the head of an elephant throwing spears, and a man in white shot lightning from his fingers. Spectacle is the closest word I can think of, but it's not even close to describing what I viewed out that window.

A long time later, the creature stumbled, then fell. The fighters swarmed over the body of the creature as the clouds covered the battlefield. We were back to flashes of colored lights. The last thing we saw before the sun went down was a dark mass of spinning clouds slowly traveling across the valley, flecked with threads of silver sparks. The mass was lit by a glowing white waterfall pouring out of its center.

The next morning began with lighter skies and thinning clouds. The storms faded during the course of the day, and the sun came out and stayed out by midafternoon. The mountain peaks were visible for the first time since we arrived. Our view was a pristine valley, with large swaths of green grass and grazing animals. Silver Station had disappeared, and we could see no sign of any other human habitation. I pulled the key from the hotel out of my pocket and stared at it. The key was now my only proof the hotel had ever existed.

The clouds began to dance after sunset, weaving in and out in a complicated pattern for hours, before twisting into a small vortex spinning upwards out of sight. Later, we were treated to a glowing river of bright greens, blues, and purples that shifted and danced on invisible winds, brighter than any aurora borealis I had ever seen.

On that last day—the eighth, if I counted right—we packed our things and prepared to leave our refuge. I opened the garage door, and we headed outside. The warm sun felt wonderful. We breathed in the fresh air, admiring the view. Our ledge was dotted with colorful clumps of yellow, pink, and purple wildflowers. They made a nice contrast to the small airy clouds in the bright blue sky. Fluffy bumped my leg with her head. "Well, Fluffy, I'm glad you were here with me to protect me and keep me company. Thank you." I scratched her behind the ears.

[*Mr. Edwards stopped, looked at me for a moment, and sighed*]

Agent Two: Is that all, Mr. Edwards?

Edwards: No, it's going to get weirder. Yes, I know how idiotic that sounds, considering what I've already told you, but it's the truth. It got weirder.

I heard ragtime music in the distance, steadily growing louder. A classic car from the early 1900s floated over the ledge and quietly landed. No engine sound, just the music. I'm not a car guy, but this was an Art Deco beauty: ivory and chocolate brown with a sloping front grille, wire-covered headlights, and large wide fenders. A gold sculpture of a winged goddess stretching to the sky had pride of place on the hood. The top was down, showing off mahogany leather seats, a burl-wood dash, and an instrument panel with gold-rimmed gauges. One gauge pulsed with orange and blue lights.

A contralto female voice in my head said, *It's a 1935 Auburn Boattail Speedster. Freya made a few modifications when she had it restored.* I turned my head to look at Fluffy, who gave the feline equivalent of a shrug.

I thought back, *Now you talk to me?*

Not much to say.

Hmph.

Freya stepped out of the car. Wow. She was a striking woman. Flawless skin and honey-blonde hair in one long braid down her back. A cream-colored sheath dress that showed off her muscular legs and arms. Her smile was strained, and she looked exhausted. "Took a long time to stop this one." She looked at the cat and smiled. "You did a good job up here, but we need to get moving and go pick up your sister."

Fluffy tilted her head, then turned away and licked her paw. Freya rolled her eyes, sighed, and said, "Yeah, yeah." She put her hand over her heart and spoke. "Oh, feline companion who pulls my chariot, you are wondrous, and amazing, and you protected your charge well. Your deeds have been entered in the journal of Mimir and written with a pen energized by Zeus. They will be recorded in the sagas and sung for the ages."

Freya put her hand down, and said, "Better, cat?" Fluffy sauntered over and rubbed against her legs. As she scratched the cat's ears, I heard her muttering about "that damn Spurgle fellow..." She looked up, the dramatic pose gone and her eyes dead serious. "Remember the name Andrew Spurgle as a lesson and a warning. We told him not to play with the Monkey God, that it would take him over and try to destroy as many humans as possible. Odin tried to talk to him, Brigid tried, and Diana tried. Even Coyote visited and talked to him. They all warned him to bury it or drop it in a volcano.

"Spurgle didn't believe them, said they were frauds and thieves trying to steal his treasure. He even said"—she made finger quotes—"'How much trouble can a little gold monkey head who grants wishes make?' He made offerings and woke the beast, certain he was smarter than the gods." She looked disgusted. "Andrew Spurgle. Stupid fecking idiot." She went still, becoming colder, her eyes changing from blue to gold, and her voice had an icy echo that made me shiver.

If someone offers you a gold monkey head inside a box made of the most perfect Sandalwood, lined with red and gold embroidered silk, don't touch it. Run like hell.

Freya blinked, and her eyes went back to their normal blue. She shook her head, smiled at me, and changed. The long braid turned into a short haircut with a thin tail. Her elegant clothes morphed into jeans and a sweater. The car stayed the same.

"Get in the car, you furry-eared feline. Time to rest up before the next crisis."

Fluffy grew to lion size, and put her paws on my shoulders. She sniffed, nuzzled then licked my face, purring. In my head, I heard, *Be well, Oren. You're not bad, for a human.*

"Any time you're ready, cat."

Fluffy disappeared in a shower of sparkles. She reappeared in her normal size on the seat next to Freya, and sat with a grumpy meow.

"You called her Fluffy?"

"Yes, I did." I shrugged and put my hands out, palm up. "We were busy and she has a lot of hair."

Freya's peal of laughter lightened the air around us, and made me smile. "Now finish packing and scoot. Coyote wants his bachelor pad back." Fluffy looked at me one last time and blinked her eyes. Then the Auburn slowly floated up and disappeared into the clouds.

I stood there on the ledge, reliving the past few days in my head. A gentle breeze brought me back to myself. Time to pick up the last items in the kitchen: my wallet, car keys, protein bars, the journal... There was an empty space on the counter where I had placed the journal, pen, and hotel key before we went outside. I searched the entire house, but they were gone.

There was nothing left for me to do but leave. As I pulled out of my refuge, the gates began to sparkle. They disappeared completely by the time my vehicle was fully on the road, and a plain dirt driveway appeared in my rearview mirror. I made my way down the mountain and marveled at the changes. No town, no gas station, no road between them, and no other buildings. I gave my information to the officers at the roadblock, then drove up to Denver and checked in to a hotel. Let my project team know I was in town and waited for my interview with the FBI.

Agent Two: Do you have anything else you want to tell us, Mr. Edwards?

Edwards: You don't believe me. I can see it in your eyes. Well, you know, I really do not care. You have my statement, and I will take a lie detector test if you want. Everything I have said is true, and the town of Silver Station is gone. Now go away and leave me alone.

END OF INTERVIEW

COLORADO INCIDENT - FINDINGS

1) Mr. Edwards's background check revealed no red flags, and he passed a voluntary polygraph test. His blood revealed no traces of narcotics or hallucinogens. A search of his hotel room revealed a small personal notebook. The last entry discussed his trip from Pagosa to Silver Station, and the people in costume he met at the Grand Silver Hotel. There was no trace of the leather journal and pen described in the interview.

2) A large green field now occupies the location of the town of Silver Station. Highway 160 stops abruptly at the edge of the field, and starts up again on the other side.

3) Agents searched the foothills of Mount Pintada, but found no trace of the garage or cave house. A large brass tag from the Grand Silver Hotel with Mr. Edwards's room number was found on the ledge of an empty lot. The hotel tag, combined with charge receipts from the hotel and gas station, tie Mr. Edwards to the area on the appropriate dates.

4) The sheriff and local police were notified when groups of Silver Station residents and tourists arrived in neighboring towns, having no memory of leaving or driving to their destination. A glowing barrier prevented physical entry to the valley. Other attempts to view the area were also unsuccessful: reconnaissance aircraft were turned aside in a different direction, and infrared satellites were unable to penetrate the clouds. All barriers vanished on day eight.

5) Three days after the incident, police found an elderly, white-haired man hiding next to a group of rocks. He was emaciated and dehydrated, does not respond to stimuli, and refuses to let go of a mangled blue backpack. Claw marks on his blue denim shirt, and his severely abraded hands and arms indicate major trauma. The man rocks and repeats, "I didn't mean to, I didn't mean to," over and over. Doctors say he may never recover, and will likely spend his life in an insane asylum.

Aside from his age, the man matches Mr. Edwards's description of Andrew Spurgle. A background check revealed a long record as a low-level grifter, moving from place to place every few months. His current whereabouts are unknown. The damage to the man's hands is too severe to obtain fingerprints. Investigators are searching for a relative to provide a DNA sample for comparison.

CONCLUSION: The town of Silver Station vanished, and we have no idea how it happened. Unless you believe Mr. Edwards.

Signed and Certified,

R.J. Allen

ASAC-Special Investigations

END MEMORANDUM

EPILOGUE

One week after his final interview with the FBI, Oren Edwards left his hotel room, picked up a large coffee, and drove to Confluence Park near the South Platte River. He sat at a picnic table and listened to the river as it rushed over the boulders, watched the children playing in the shallow water and the families enjoying a cookout.

Oren thought about the old-fashioned hotel key hanging around his neck, and how much his life had changed. He remembered removing and dropping the brass tag after Freya left, hiding the hotel key in plain sight on his personal key ring.

He thought of Freya, and the parts he did not share with the FBI.

"Oh, feline companion who pulls my chariot, you are wondrous, and amazing, and you protected your bard well."

Wait, what? I'm a bard?

Hush. Later.

He thought of Fluffy's last words. *Be well, Bard Oren. You're not bad, for a human.*

He smiled, and thought of the gray and white long-haired kitten who jumped on his chest two mornings ago. As he scratched the purring kitten, he heard, *You may NOT name him Fluffy. Any other name is acceptable. Treat your new companion well.*

Yes, that was definitely Fluffy's voice. A warm contralto, sounding annoyed. He heard Fluffy's voice once more, after naming the kitten. *Bruno? Really?*

He looked up at the ceiling, saying out loud, "He likes it. You have a better name, cat?" Bruno meowed, loudly.

Hmph. Fine.

"Thank you, Fluffy."

A new journal and pen arrived with the kitten, along with a leather cord for the key. A note was tucked inside the journal:

If you decide to walk down this path, you will need training. Contact us at this number when you are ready.

Under the telephone number, Freya had penned, *Come on up to Valhalla and visit us sometime.*

He returned from his memories, scanning his surroundings. No one was paying attention to him or the kitten playing at his feet. Oren C. Edwards pulled out the leather journal, opened it, and removed the pen cap with a small black lightning bolt.

Sipping his coffee, he began to write.

To Whom it May Concern

Kortnee Bryant

Dear Sir or Madam:

I am writing to you today to explain, as requested, the events that occurred on the afternoon of the thirteenth of July, surrounding the loss of my assistant and the subsequent termination of the lease of apartment 413.

Of note is that the washing machine had been the subject of several work orders, all entered, approved and dispatched to Andrew Spurgle, who is no longer with the company. Records seem to indicate he was terminated for job abandonment and has been reported missing.

The work order we had been sent to fulfill had been outstanding for quite some time, with calls from the tenant coming more frequently, the last several being marked as urgent. The washing machine had stopped working and there was standing water. Under normal circumstances, anything that is water-related is taken care of immediately, as running water can cause structural damages and standing water is a health hazard.

Andrew Spurgle was the maintenance engineer onsite for the first report. Unfortunately, there was nobody who was qualified to fulfill the work order, as all of the maintenance staffers who had experience fixing a washing machine had quit or been fired recently. As there was nobody qualified to fulfill the work order, the work order went unfulfilled.

When the tenant sent a letter and a bill from an emergency trip to the hospital for allergic reactions directly related to the standing water in her washing machine, the apartment manager began interviewing people to fill the maintenance spots that were open, paying close attention to the people who were qualified or willing to become qualified to fix washing machines.

Also, the tenant's husband came by and politely and firmly requested someone be sent to fix the standing water in the washing machine. That the man was approximately six feet, five inches tall and looked as though he played defense for the local football team was merely a fact that was noted in case he became violent. As the entire encounter was polite, bordering on genial, it should be noted here that we were, in fact, noting it at the time.

Realizing the urgency of the problem, one of my assistants and myself undertook to at least drain the water from the broken washing machine. In this instance, we judged that a shop-vac would be of use, and I was to carry and dump said shop-vac after my assistant had filled it. The closest drain was the tenant's bathtub, and that was deemed an appropriate place to dump the shop-vac.

When we reached the apartment, the tenant greeted us, and she did look as though she was suffering badly from some kind of allergy. She directed us to the washing machine and stood back to observe us as we worked.

I positioned myself in the middle of the bathroom doorway and plugged in the shop-vac. My assistant opened the door to the closet the washing machine was stored in. The smell that was released when the washing machine was opened was the most horrid thing I had ever encountered in my life to that point. It was at that point that I noticed the line of air fresheners stored on top of the toilet tank and was surprised at how well they'd worked to keep the stench at bay.

My assistant determined that the cause of the problem was an electrical short that had kept the controls from working. There was no solution short of replacing the whole washing machine that we could determine, but we also agreed that the water needed to be drained from the machine before it could be replaced. My assistant turned on the shop-vac and began to suck up the water. When the hose was clogged almost immediately, he pulled it out to see if it had been caught on anything that had been left in the machine, as we had been given to understand that she had been in the middle of washing a load of towels and had not been able to remove everything. Not finding a cause for the clog, my assistant turned the shop-vac back on and continued to remove the water. When the hose clogged again, my assistant leaned over the water to try and see if there was anything in the machine that he could remove.

It was at that point that the tentacles shot out of the machine and grabbed my assistant. Stunned with shock, it took a moment for the tenant and myself to react. My assistant was fighting the pull of the tentacles, and they were bigger than anything that should have been able to fit in the washing machine. Nothing we did was able to force the tentacles to release their hold on my assistant and they pulled him into the machine, head-first. Having pulled my assistant into the machine, the tentacles retracted and the washing machine stopped moving. It is my greatest hope that he drowned before the creature ate him.

Recovering slightly from the shock, the tenant said, "Fuck this" and began packing a bag. She informed me that she would return with several large men to get the rest of her things, but she would not be living in the unit any longer.

I locked the front door on my way back to the office to report on our attempt to fulfill the work order and to let the manager know we would need to hire another maintenance staffer.

Since this event, there have been two exterminators lost to the creature in the washing machine and another member of the maintenance staff.

It is my recommendation that someone with experience be contacted to discover the nature of the creature, the best way to get rid of it, and where to find a washing machine repairman willing to work for an apartment complex. I have attached a business card for a detective I have been referred to.

Yours truly,

TO WHOM IT MAY CONCERN

Julio Martinez, Maintenance Manager, Twin Pines Apartments

Also From Raconteur Press

Ghosts of Malta
Knights of Malta
Saints of Malta
Falcons of Malta
Space Cowboys
Space Cowboys 2: Electric Rodeo
Space Cowboys 3: Return of the Bookaroo
Space Cowboys 404: Cow Not Found
Space Marines
Space Marines 2
PinUp Noir
PinUp Noir 2
Your Honor, I Can Explain...
You See, What Happened Was...
He Was Dead When I Got There...
All Will Burn
All Will Burn: Fierce Love
Moggies in Space
Moggies Back in Space
Full Steam Ahead
Giant! Freakin'! Robots!

Call To Action

At Raconteur Press, our motto is Have Fun, Get Paid. Hopefully you enjoyed the stories in this volume. If you did, please take the time to leave a quick review. Our authors love to hear that people enjoyed their stories and it encourages them to write more of them.

And if you liked a story by a particular author, go ahead and find their author page and give them a follow to get notifications about their next release. It might be with Raconteur Press or it might not but it'll probably be another fantastic story.

Enjoy our stories?

Want to see more of them?

Leave a review!

It's like a hug without all that awkward eye contact

Made in the USA
Columbia, SC
21 March 2024